A Life Without Consequences

BY STEPHEN ELLIOTT

Names have not been changed to protect the innocent.
There are no innocent.

A Life Without Consequences

BY STEPHEN ELLIOTT

MacAdam/Cage

MacAdam/Cage Publishing
155 Sansome Street, Suite 550
San Francisco, CA 94104
www.macadamcage.com

Library of Congress Cataloging-in-Publication Data

Elliott, Stephen, 1971 —
  A Life Without Consequences / by Stephen Elliott.
    p. cm.
  ISBN: 0-9673701-7-5 (alk. paper)
  ISBN: 1-931561-19-2 (alk. paper)
    1. Teenage boys — Fiction. 2. Homeless teenagers — Fiction. 3. Maternal deprivation — Fiction. 4. Chicago (Ill.)— Fiction. 5. Group homes — Fiction
I. Title.

PS3605.L45 L5 2001
813'.3 — dc21   2001037019

Manufactured in the United States of America.

10 9 8 7 6 5 4 3 2 1

Book design by Dorothy Carico Smith.

This book is dedicated to Maria Duryea and her family:
Josie, J. Bob, Bennie, Annette, Michelle, Connor, Jake and Chrissy Bell.
Thanks for the bed in the basement and the ensuing holiday turkeys.

1. ENTER

I roll on the couch, silent like padded footsteps. A dirty blue pillow softens my cheek. My mind is half white, half black. I roll in the couch, still asleep, still a child. The light from the window paints a pink haze under my eyelids.

It's raining blows. Raining blows like so many moons on so many homeless nights, it's raining blows.

I try to stop the fists by raising my forearm over my head. My father is screaming, spit flying out of his mouth and onto mine. He's screaming and he's hitting me but his fists are not as strong and I'm covering my face until he grabs me by the hair and pulls me into the empty kitchen, my knees on the yellow linoleum floor. This kitchen was our kitchen. I grew up here. Then one day my mother died, I left home, and my father moved into a big house with his new wife out in the suburbs.

He sees where I put my cigarette out on the floor and smacks my face open-handed. "You deserve it," he tells me as if to convince himself. I sit in front of him, my knees sheathed in frayed and torn blue jeans I've been wearing for a month. On my knees facing the naked cabinets, bowed like a present for my father, the gift of his little boy. "You're an animal," he tells me. "You're a pig."

I hear the hum of the clippers start. He's had them here, he's prepared. He left the house waiting for me like a net. Waiting for me to crawl in from the cold, like an animal.

My hair falls, leaves to the floor. Far away a siren gets louder and then disappears. A brick sits in my stomach, a ball of twine in my throat. My hair litters the bright linoleum floor stained by the sun pouring through the window.

I am bald now. My punishment. My father lays his clippers on the countertop. "Go take a shower." In the bathroom I look at my face: a small black eye. I run my fingers over my head. I'm not bald, my head is covered with quarter-inch peach fuzz and in the back I can feel my scalp where the clippers slipped. Two square patches, like a mental patient.

I climb out of the bathroom window, one last look at the old house. From the outside broken yellow stucco and a bright green lawn. A bright green sign on the corner says, "Coyle Ave." It's so bright and sunny, it's six in the morning. I know on the other side of the house there's a trail of vomit from what used to be my bedroom window. I walk down the street, the sun beating on the square patches of my scalp, into a day.

There's a festival in Warren Park, "Taste of the 50th." They sell cheese pizza and hot dogs and polish sausages under wide yellow tents. There are live bands and I walk around asking people to buy me beers. I can't buy my own beers, I have no money, and I'm only 14.

The park smells of grass and sausage. I approach a large man with a long beard and skinny legs. "Fuck off, man. I don't even know you."

Another guy buys me a beer. I tell him I need a place to sleep tonight. He looks away and says, "Look, I bought you a beer."

The crowd is thin and I sit on the hill listening to music, feeling sorry for myself. As the day wears on the crowds get thicker, the music angrier. I join a slam dance pit, ramming into people, trying to hit them with my head, angry, my jeans swaying, almost falling off drunk, dizzy, closer to the stage, louder, faster, harder, more, louder, faster, harder, more.

Now I am in a hallway bleeding to death. My wrist is slashed wide open, I am a victim of my own violence. I haven't been happy.

People walk into the hallway, going to their apartments. They step over me and I look up at them with one eye. It's late, someone is always awake somewhere. Finally the light comes shining through the door, circling, spinning and turning the hallway into a five-by-ten disco. The Angel of Law. I start to get up and think better of it. "Fuck'em."

The black boots step into the hallway, Clack, Clack, two of them, a man and a woman. His moustache droops over his fat, happy cheeks. Her thighs bulge in her tight cop pants, creasing between her legs. Large breasts under cop leather.

"How old are you?"

"Fourteen."

"Where are your parents?"

"I don't know."

"What do you mean 'you don't know'?"

I shrug my shoulders, stare down at the dried blood on the hallway floor. I'm not going to die. Damn.

At the station they leave me in a small room to wait for the juvenile police. I sit on a scratched metal cot. I lie down and the metal is cold on my naked head. The juvenile cops come in, again a man and a woman. They look beaten and wear old clothes filled with wrinkles.

He asks, "Are you hungry?"

She asks, "What's that hole in your wrist?"

"Sure," I reply. "Can I smoke?"

The lady hands me a cigarette, raises her eyebrows. I pull on the cigarette, taste the smoke, touch my face. My face is covered in acne. I know I'm ugly and I hate myself for it.

"Well?" she asks.

"I fell on a tin can."

She lights a cigarette for herself. Her fingernails are stained with tobacco smoke. The man gets up, walks out of the room.

She crosses, uncrosses her legs. I tap my fingers on the steel cot, shift my weight and begin to count the bricks. "So you don't know where your family is?"

"I know where my mother is," I tell her. "She's dead."

"How long?"

"'Bout a year. Less."

She nods, pulls. "What about your father?"

I shrug my shoulders. "He moved. Trying to sell his old house I guess, but there's a cigarette stain on the kitchen floor."

"You know where he moved to?"

"Suburbs. I don't know. He didn't tell me." I finger the back of my head. Can feel the cool tips of my fingers.

"How long have you been living on the streets?"

"'Bout a year."

"About the time your mom died?"

"'Bout that time."

The male cop comes back in, hands me a sandwich, a slice of baloney between two dry pieces of bread. I take a bite and chew slowly; bread, meat, it's too much. I throw up into the small brown trashcan.

"We're going to take you to the hospital where they're going to give you a checkup. Then we're going to find a place for you to stay. OK?"

"OK."

I'm tired. I'm so tired. The nurse has taken my blood pressure, she's ran her tests, she's told me that the hole in my arm is not from a can. The cut is too clean.

"Why would you do that?" she asks.

"Why wouldn't I do that?" I ask back.

She shakes her head. She's pretty. I'm ugly. She's like every other person that never asked me to move in with them. Like every teacher in my school who would buy me a forty-cent lunch but nothing more. They all knew I slept on a rooftop on the corner of California and Devon. They all knew I was sleeping over the store that sold fake leathers and furs to people that couldn't afford real leather and furs. The teachers knew, the crossing guard knew, the lady that worked the counter at the diner knew, her husband the cop knew, the neighbors knew, the Indians that run the corner store knew, people I didn't even know knew. And all the parents in the PTA kept telling their kids to keep away from me, I'm a bad influence, a drug addict.

"That's like all the rest," I tell her. She looks at me sadly and says nothing more. She leaves me in the room. "You gonna take me home?" I say.

Reed is located behind a wrought-iron fence, nine feet high, on the northwest side of Chicago. Rolling Stone Records is close by, with thirty-foot cardboard cutouts of Mick Jagger and Iggy Pop. I used to hang out at Rolling Stone with my friends and listen to heavy metal tapes and wear T-shirts that said 'Metal Up Your Ass!' But I never went inside the gates of Reed. Lawns roll over the grounds, spotted and patchy. Functional brick buildings dot the landscape, a basketball court with one rim missing. Quiet, empty, mystical, lost.

My caseworker drives. I just met her this morning. She pulls at tawny gray hairs tied up in a bun. We drive deeper; the sun passes behind some clouds. A Bible sits on her dashboard, thin, leather-bound, and cracked. Now a park in front of a large white building, people walk slowly like at a large picnic. Some of them wear helmets and drool down their shirts. A small group of men and women in white shirts sit near the back, smiling. We come around the building over a black asphalt road. To the right, small red brick buildings with windows broken out hidden by trees close by the outer gate. "The back wards," she whispers. The road curves, seeming to continue out of nothing, here and there glimpses of the street, and finally we stop in front of a rusted steel sign, filthy with dirt, sticking out of the ground five feet with small block letters proclaiming, "Henry Horner Children's Adolescent Center."

She smiles at me, the thin smile cracking her face. "Well, here we are."

"Here we are." I kick my toe into the dirt.

"We've arrived."

"I've arrived, you're going home."

"They're going to ask you questions. Just try to be honest. This is not a punishment for something you've done wrong." She tries to give me a look that says 'trust me,' but it doesn't and I don't. "You may not believe it, but people want to help you."

"I may not believe it," I agree. We close the doors and I walk inside with her behind the locked curtain.

The psychiatrist wants to know if I have allergies, if I take any medication. I tell him I have hay fever. He rubs his bald head; I rub mine. His window is covered with mesh grating and outside it's starting to rain. He pages through his manual with a large thumb absently, not really looking for anything. I can feel the rain in my bones. My bones feel wet. I spent a lot of cold wet nights over the last year, huddled under box tops, hiding in boiler rooms, running, and running.

"I'm going to prescribe you something for your allergies."

"Alright."

"Actifed. That's all. A decongestant." I nod. I feel slow, sad. "Are you hungry?" he asks. I think about the baloney sandwich choking my throat until I turn blue. I laugh just for a second, just to keep back the tears.

Sometimes days and nights, light and dark, just run together into a thick soup and time moves while standing still. My first days at Reed are this way, clouded in a mind-numbing depression, unable to move, conquered by a complete stillness. The world could stop and I would float off into space and never notice. When it ends it's like coming out of a coma, but one that will always return, always has.

It's been a long year. Started with Mother's death. She's lying in bed, mostly bone white but deep red and purple on one side of her body where all her blood has pooled. It was a long time in coming and nothing to be surprised by. My best friend Justin waited for me down by the canal with bottles of cheap vodka and pills and I drank and I forgot. He held onto me and said don't think about it and I said don't worry, I won't.

I tie my sheets under my bed, pull the ends tighter and then knot them so I don't have to remake my bed every morning. Fall comes in dark rumbling highways, thick black clouds plastering the sky through a screened-in window that opens diagonally exactly six inches.

I wiggle my toes inside a pair of ripped-up Converse, basketball star. My feet are too wide, the shoes are too old. My roommates are in school. I can't go to school because I'm on runaway alert. I should have been starting high school in two days. I never would have gone anyway.

Here it's quiet. The ceiling is made of flat cardboard slats and square florescent lights. Each room contains four beds. The bathrooms are across the hall from my room, they have no doors on the stalls. When my roommate Jay goes to the bathroom he shits with the only towel in the place over his crotch so no one can see his dirty yellow pubic hairs.

I move slowly; no one is waiting for me. My mouth tastes like day-old beer but it's been a week. I smooth the sheet with my palm, take in the stark white walls dark ribbons running along the cracks, taste the overly sanitized odor lurking through the hallways. Everything's chemical; everything's wrong.

Jay and French Fry beat each other with the plastic ends of the Connect Four games until their shoulders start to bleed. They sit on the beds, exhausted, sweat pouring out of their hair. They both smile. Jay because he's impressed with himself, French Fry because he's impressed Jay.

"I'm a Satanist," Jay tells me.

"That's cool." I'm wearing the same shirt I wore a week ago when my father caught me in his house and shaved my head. It says Zoetrope. It's the name of a heavy metal band. Jay has long stringy blond hair.

"You've got the most fucked up haircut I've ever seen," Jay tells me.

"It used to be longer."

"When Mike saw you in intake he laughed at those patches in the back of your head. They make you look crazy."

"Yeah." I tap my legs. Jay smiles, each end of his mouth sticking past his ears. "Well, we're in a mental hospital," I let him know.

"You think you can kick my ass?" Jay asks.

"I don't care."

"You think you could kick Mike's ass."

"I could kick Mike's ass all over the place," I tell him. French Fry falls back on himself.

"Damn!" The bloodied ends of the game sit by Jay's bed, the tattered box in front on the floor. French Fry shakes and holds his stomach, his horrible skin scarred and creased. He tried to burn himself to death but failed. Mike took pills. Jay burned down a church. Mostly it's attempted suicides. A big zoo full of morons. We don't know any better.

They hand out little plastic cups full of green shampoo for our showers. Some kid always sits in the bathtub and Jay always spits on him when he goes to shower. Jay will shower until they tell him he has to leave, trying to get clean, there is no soap, only shampoo. But the shampoo sticks to our skin and so Jay stays under the water trying to get the shampoo off. Finally, he turns the rusted tap with his long, skinny fingers.

We don't have heat but we have thin blankets. French Fry piles them on ten thick. "I'm not cold," he tells me. "I like heat." There are moments when I want to touch French Fry's horrible face, all scarred and nearly burnt to death. When I want to kiss him with my tongue just for being so unbearably ugly. For being the ugliest human being I've ever seen.

Reed is not a place for the beautiful. Jay says he wants to be a model. He's skinny and tall with long hair, dry like horse rope, and his stomach muscles poke out of him like pebbles.

Molly is beautiful. Molly lives on the outside, behind the screened-in windows and bolted doors and thirteen-foot fence. Molly is my primary. My therapist.

Molly squints when she smiles. She has thick legs, a short body, a big ass. On the outside she's just another woman in a long skirt. In here she's more.

I stare at her legs when she talks, daydreaming about getting between them, about sliding up between her feet, her knees, until I crawl inside of her completely and go to sleep.

"You have a twitch," she says. "Right over your nose."

"Sometimes I'm nervous."

"I read your file."

"You must have a lot of time on your hands."

Molly smiles. I play with the frays on my jeans, hunch my back, touch my knees. I can be like an ogre.

"Your father used to beat you."

"You could say that."

"How often?"

"A few times. It could of been worse. Mostly it was verbal." I look up, she's squinting. Fuck. It's like talking to an absence. "He shaved my head a couple of times. Handcuffed me to a pipe."

Molly nods. I look at her feet; she's wearing blue nylons. Papers and books stack the wall behind her and next to us a big window with not much to see. Molly squints. "Do you think you're looking for a mother figure? Someone to replace your mother?"

"My mother didn't do anything but sit on the couch and die for five years. I don't want to replace that." A silence hangs over us for a few minutes. I play with my fingers, stare at my folded hands. Her floor is the same as every floor in the hospital. A calendar hangs over her desk with a picture of a dove with its wings spread. A Bible sits by the window, the same cracked Bible that was in the car.

"You're very intelligent for your age." I shrug my shoulders, think to myself: I'm smarter than you. "You talk like an adult."

"I write poetry," I blurt out. Damn. I look at her ankles, then up at her shoulders.

"Look at me," she says. Her eyes shine, she squints. "I'd like to read your poetry." I shrug my shoulders. Her ankles. Time's up. We stand, shake hands. "We'll talk next week." Her hands are soft.

I'm lying on my bed when Mr. Macy comes to get me. Mr. Macy is a large black man. He walks with one leg far out in front of the other, a hand in his pocket. He leads me down the hall.

"You like to play chess?" he asks me. I don't answer him. I don't feel like lightening the mood. "Don't like chess, huh. What about basketball? You watch Bulls games?" Still no answer. "How about big titties? You like big fat titties?" I can't help but laugh and look up into his big smiling face. Mr. Macy takes me into the small room off of the TV room. My father sits there with his new wife. She has good legs and an overbite. I walk around them, sit back towards the window. More views of nothing. He motions to a stack of newspapers and magazines on the pale gray table. He has thick fingers, large hands. I spy my own fingers, my own hands.

"I thought you would want to read these. That you might be bored." I can't look at him. "You're free to come home anytime."

"Where is that?" I ask him.

"You'll find out."

I put my head in my hands, rub my face. Molly tells me I twitch, I know I twitch. Now I'm sitting across from my twitch. "Here Paul," my stepmother says. Mr. Macy watches from the corner of the doorway frame. She hands me a plastic watch. I spy her overbite, her forearm coming out of a T-shirt, father's jowls, big hands, big teeth. I hang the watch in front of me by its strap and pitch it into the dull green metal can where it dies with a thud.

"I wonder if I could piss on you from here," I tell my father.

"It's been hard for all of us."

"You told my mother she wasn't a fit mother."

"Don't tell me that," his voice rising. "You killed your mother. The way you treated her. Always badgering her for money to support your drug habit."

"You told her that when you got married you had a bargain, and she wasn't living up to her end of the bargain. Is your new wife living up to the bargain? What's it been?"

He talks more, answers me back, something loud and angry. He's going to beat me, he says. Next time with a belt. Tells me again I killed my mother. He's wrong, though. Multiple Sclerosis killed my mother, any fool knows that. Knows that one day she didn't wake up, that all the blood had floated to one side of her body and settled in a big blue pool and the rest of her body was just white. I couldn't do that, which is how I know that I didn't kill her. I just rub my fingers over the bumps on my face. "You make me sick," I tell him and walk out of the room and into the TV room and sit in front of the TV on the plastic couch. I hear the large metal door close and I know he is gone.

"I'd like you to get a test done," Molly tells me. Today she wears green, a green velvet skirt, green tights. "It's to see if you're depressed."

"I am depressed," I tell her. "I've been depressed for a long time."

"I know. We just want to measure your depression."

"You'd be depressed too if you'd slept on rooftops for the last year."

"I know." She says it but she doesn't know anything.

Molly leans back, her golden hair moves along her shoulders under the light. I'm depressed and I'm tired. A book sits on her desk titled *Higher Education*. A thought occurs to me.

"Where is the University of Chicago?" I ask her.

"It's on the South Side." She gets comfortable, leans forward over the table. "It's a very good school."

"Did you go there?"

"No. I went to Circle Campus and received my social work degree at DePaul."

"Why didn't you go to the University of Chicago?"

"It's a very good school. It's very hard to get in."

"I think I'd like to go to the University of Chicago."

Molly squints. "I think you're very bright Paul. You could do whatever you want to do."

She doesn't know anything. You can't just do whatever you want. Maybe some people can. "You're Mike's therapist too, right?"

"Yes."

"You like him."

"Of course."

I nod. She crosses her legs.

"Could Mike do anything he wants too?"

"If he puts his mind to it."

"How much do you get paid?" I ask her. She squints.

"I can't tell you that."

"I should be in school. Otherwise I'll never make it to a university."

"OK. I'll take you off the runaway list."

"Good. Because I'm tired of sitting on plastic couches watching TV while the crazies try to punch holes in the walls."

"Don't worry, Paul. I'll take you off the runaway list."

Jay, Mike, and I smoke a joint in the bedroom. I start school tomorrow. We try to be careful and blow our smoke out the window but the window doesn't open far. It's cold in the room and French Fry is asleep under all of his blankets. I listen for coyotes outside.

Mike smuggled the joint back after a home visit he had last weekend. He was lucky. He got Ziggy and Ziggy doesn't strip search. Mike won't be going home though. He tried to kill his stepdad and soon they'll put him in a group home. "So Jay says you think you can kick my ass," Mike says through a cloud of smoke. A figure passes in the hallway, a dark silhouette against the yellow light.

"That's true," I say.

"You think you're hot shit but you're not."

"I don't think I'm hot shit," I tell Mike. "I don't care at all."

"When my father died I laughed and laughed," says Jay. The pot feels nice. I don't understand why they don't just pass it out. It has to be safer than Thorazine or Haldal. The other day I took Myafsky's Thorazine for him. He's six-six and I was hallucinating on the walls and when it was over I was so surprised.

"I'll whoop your ass," Mike says.

"I'll punch you in the lip and make you look like a duck," I tell him, and Jay coughs on his smoke and the three of us burst out laughing and then stop when the silhouette passes in the hall, again.

We sit stoned on the edges of the beds. Out the window a silent darkness winds through the grounds. "I've never seen so much nothing," I say and then Jay says, "Quack, quack," and Mike punches me in the eye.

I roll off the bed. Mike charges and I move aside and his head hits the wall. I wrap my arm around his head in a headlock while Jay laughs and shakes like a hyena. I bang Mike's head into the wall a few more times while he swings blindly and knocks my face.

I push him away and we stand up. "It's cool," Mike says. There's a bloodstain on the wall from his head.

"Alright." We sit back down.

"You're OK," Mike tells me.

"You're OK, too." Jay goes to sleep in the dark room and Mike and I sit for a while contemplating our wounds.

Winter is coming in, frosting the grass between the dorm and the school. In the morning we are woken and then marched along a thin path watched by the lazy eyes of the staff. Does the rest of the world know about these forgotten brick buildings buried deep in Chicago? Do they know about the shit on the walls?

I test into the top class in the school, a level above Mike and Jay. But it doesn't matter; my teacher, with his perfectly groomed beard, is nothing more than a babysitter and his five students sit at a long table, and sometimes fight.

"Tanya, give me some love."

Tanya is dark, black, with large breasts. I don't know what she did to end up in this netherworld. She's quiet, older than I am. I know she did something bad.

"Why?" she asks.

"Because, Tanya. Somebody has to love me. Got a family?"

"No."

"Me either."

We draw on construction paper. I draw swirls and tiny mushroom clouds. Tanya fills the page with bright orange birds.

After lunch Mike, Jay and I hide out in the bathroom with a paper bag and a small jar of liquid paper.

"I heard you were hitting on that nigger," Jay says, trying not to let out too much breath.

"Nigger lover," Mike says.

"It's a small world in here," I try to explain, but it's a weak explanation so I drop the subject.

Just before leaving school for the day I get Tanya to lift her shirt up under the table and I touch her nipples with the back of my fingers. It's the first time I've ever touched a girl's breasts. They are magic.

We sit in the conference room, Jay, Mike, French Fry, myself, a few others. Molly sits in front of us and behind her a blackboard. Staff stands on either side, frozen in time. The walls run yellow and shades of green. Off to my left, the TV room. This place is not large, Molly is doing something with her hair, assuming an authority.

"We know you have been smoking pot in the residence." I look at my hands. Jay looks around like he's bored. "And it's a crime, a crime in here, just like anywhere." Here they have their own security guards and I wonder how they would feel about being replaced with real cops. They don't get called to the adolescent unit much, we're a drugged-up bunch, quiet, easy to handle. Molly's skirt just passes her knees.

"You don't know about suffering," mumbles Fry. "I've seen hell," he looks up from under his eyelids. "I've burnt in hell." His burnt face stares forward. Molly half squints. It's not over.

"This is not about heaven or hell," and I wait for her to say his name but she doesn't. "This is about right and wrong. This is about the law. And this won't be tolerated."

"You have no proof," I say.

"Be quiet, Paul." I look down. I look at her shoes. I dream of the walls in her office. There is more talk. It's nothing though. Out the window, I have an urge to leave. My chest hurts. Not to my room, to the outside. Perhaps I could drive out one night with Molly, my head in her lap under her steering wheel. Maybe Tanya will leave with me, we'll escape together.

Like a conference of elders, Jay, Mike, French Fry, and I sit on the confining couch under the television, speaking in muted half-tones. "How do they know we're smoking pot in the room?" Mike asks.

"Someone saw," I suggest.

"Someone told," Mike counters. "How do we know you're not a spy, that you're really a patient at all? Maybe you're staff. Maybe you work here."

Behind us the room stretches out and off the left end of the rec room, the pool room. The would-be Black Gangster Disciples, Latin Kings hang out there. Crazy gangbanger would-be killers. Too weird and crazy to place in the jail so they hide them here, give them to us.

"So what you're saying is I was hired to spy on you," I say.

"That doesn't make sense," French Fry says.

"What do you know? You big ugly pizza. Now I can't go this weekend so I can't get any pot." Staff comes walking by real close then walks away. "What about that?"

"We'll have to be more careful." I still have to see Molly in the morning, and I don't know what I'll say.

Today when I meet with Molly she is stern. I sit down on the brown chair; she leans back in hers. Outside the window two men hold down a young struggling boy, waiting for a nurse to come. She smoothes her skirt. I touch my knee, still naked. I've been here a month and they haven't gotten me a pair of jeans. The silence is over-whelming. On her desk a yellow folder with my name on it.

"That my file?" I nod towards it.

"Yes."

"Can I see it?"

"No." We wait. "It's my file, my notes."

"But it's about me."

"But it's my notes."

I nod. There's a steady electric hum. I spy the outlets.

"I'm wondering about this weekend."

"You mean about you and the others being caught smoking pot?"

"Yes."

"It's very serious." She smoothes her skirt again. I lift my finger off my knee and move towards her, but it is just a moment, it passes, imperceptible.

"I wonder what that does for us." The folder on her desk, there are so many papers, but the folder on the desk. Maybe she was looking at it, preparing for our meeting. Or maybe she put it out there to taunt me, to taunt me with a folder full of lies that I can't see. Unless I pushed past her, pushed her chair over and stepped over her legs and grabbed the folder. Then, a few words before staff barreled through the door. Today she wears creamy stockings. "I wonder about us," I continue.

"What do you mean?"

I pull my shoulders up, the air is tight. "I wonder what this means."

"You mean do I still like you?" she asks, the beginning of a squint forming under her blond hair. She looks like she is about to laugh. The air is so painful I can't reply. "I still like you."

"That's good," and I want to say more but I can't, my tongue sticks. Molly uncrosses her legs and leans forward, a bit, imperceptible, perhaps. She leans forward from her chair, I sit still, frozen in time. Shortly, a silence sustained. We stand like ballet dancers and Molly leads me back to the ward and turns and I stand inside and the door closes, a small click, and the door is locked.

I play chess with Mr. Macy while Jay and Mike and thirty other residents hover by the pool table. Yesterday two people escaped: Guys from the other end of the hall. Mr. Macy pushes a black pawn. He always sets up the same. Two guys got out, hammering night after night at the wire beyond the window until it came off and then pushing and it was open. They must have smelled the air for a second, to see if it was the same. I push my knight, I'm going to attack him. They ran across the fields and no one was there and they scaled the posts and now they're gone.

"What about Jay?" I ask Mr. Macy. He raises an intelligent brow. He works evenings. I guess in his neighborhood this is considered a good job.

"Jay is a political prisoner," he tells me, pushing his bishop, a tiny whoosh of air across the old board. I nod in agreement. "You probably don't even need to be here," he tells me and he probably believes it. Of course I have secrets. Yesterday I sat in bed and cried with my hands behind my head and I couldn't think of any good reason, just cried. I can't tell him that. Maybe he has his problems as well. I notice his smooth black fingers when he moves a piece. Maybe he wears women's clothes or likes to be beaten on or harbors some homicidal intention. I don't know what jacket he is wearing on the inside. Maybe I don't need to be here.

I beat Mr. Macy today. I beat him because his opening is always the same so now I always beat him. When we first played he always beat me, but he didn't adjust. He rubs his chin; it is not shaven. I don't think he has a good job. He is not like the therapists, educated, here by choice. He is more like the prisoners, like us. Here because he has nowhere else to go. It's true that he is paid to be here, to watch after us, and protect us from ourselves. Still, what are his options?

I don't disappear with Jay and Mike today to sniff liquid paper. I disappear with Tanya and we go in a closet downstairs by the gym. "They don't watch us very well," I tell her. She shakes her head no. "I guess they figure we are good as got." I unbutton her pants, my fingers are shaking. I've never been with a girl before. Here we are all crazy and I'm starting to think that's not so bad for me because I know how ugly I am and how no girl would want to be with me out in the world.

"Run away with me," Tanya whispers through the closet. It's so dark in here and she is so dark that her voice comes from my fingers touching her, soft and quiet. I take pause for a moment. We could run away, I know it. I could run away from anything. But outside, what would I be to her? Outside where it's not so normal to drool on yourself, in a world not artificially slowed down by Haldal and Thorazine, what could I be to her out there?

I stroke her hair, pulled back tight as it is. Run my hand over it, touch her face; she has bad skin too. I shake my head but I know it's too dark for her to see me. In a few minutes we'll be officially missing. Staff will come searching the bathrooms, the closets. "We have to go back," I whisper.

"Take care of me." It lingers in the room, in the tiny room. Echoes. I have her here. Back in class I'll carve under the table when no one is looking, I'll carve, 'trust', to admonish myself. But now, I'm fourteen, locked up. We have to go back.

I grab her fingers with my fingers. She squeezes as hard as she can. I don't know what she thinks I can do. I pull her out of the closet, the light from the hall strikes us, searing. I pull her quickly and we run through the hallway, past Jay and Mike leaving the bathroom, and into class.

I've stopped thinking about windows, about outside, about options. At night my demons come out. I hear French Fry rustling underneath ten thin blankets and Jay wheezing. And I hear the empty bed too.

I sat with French Fry earlier in the rec room at a rounded table just far enough from the TV that never ended, that never shut up. "You're the Saint of Swing," French Fry told me. "You go from hot to cold. Your moods. You have to find stability. I found it. Now I'm always hot."

I touched his arm when he said it and his skin was warm. I measured him for a reaction.

"What about cocaine?" I asked him, drawing my hand away, trying to laugh a little.

"You still come down," he said. "And besides, you've never been able to afford it."

When he said that I looked over just in time to see this black kid, George, smack Mike with a pool cue and the pool cue broke and flew off into two pieces and I thought, 'Damn, no more pool.' Mike slumped to the ground in a mass.

That was this morning, and I felt fine. Now my face and pillow are soaked in stale tears. I half try to make out something in the darkness. Something beyond the sounds and the smells.

Finally I dream. I dream I'm a bartender in an oversized white shirt with tight black pants. The customers crowd the bar and clamor for shots and I line up the tiny glasses. I read their blank faces, a crowd filled with cops and abusive parents and dirty old men looking for young hitchhikers down America's highways and byways. I tip the bottle and nothing comes out and I pour them all shots of perfect nothing. I give them nothing at all but they all tip their glasses, and drink it down. And I wait for someone to choke on it, but no one does.

In school the teacher sits in front of a clean chalkboard with a book open on his wooden desk and we all kind of sit, writing in workbooks, or pretending to write in workbooks, or not pretending. Just not doing anything. Tanya pushes me a note across the table and I look to see if the teacher has looked up and he hasn't.

"My parents died in a fire," it reads.

I scribble a note back, "I know someone who tried to burn himself to death," and push it to her.

"French Fry," she lips. I nod. I touch her foot with my foot under the table, then I think about my torn-up jeans and pull my foot back. She passes me a note, 'What happened to your parents?'

"I don't care," I mouth back. Then we get back to our workbooks. I write some lines, some poetry. Something about being locked up against my will, but I know it's not true so I scratch it out. I look over at Tanya's book and she is drawing a picture of a woman in a wedding dress. It's not a bad picture. I can't draw anything. I've never been able to draw or paint.

Class breaks and people get up to go to the bathroom, or walk down the hallway, or disappear into thin air for ten minutes before coming back to this room and sitting for an hour more. The teacher closes his book, smiles as if he understands something special and we should appreciate him for it, and he leaves the room.

"Look," I say to Tanya. "my father caught me sleeping in his house and shaved my head and that's why I have this terrible haircut."

"I don't mind it."

"It's terrible because I didn't fight back. I could've run away. He's not persistent but I was too scared, so I sat on the floor and let him do this to me. I'm a coward."

"You're not a coward."

"Whatever."

"I started that fire," Tanya says. Now time stops. Time stops, pregnant. Tanya closes her eyes halfway. I hear a hum, like a funeral choir. I wonder if Jay and Mike are off with another bottle of glue. Tanya shades in the wedding dress on her picture.

"Damn," I say. "You're no coward." She blushes slightly on her dark black cheeks. I touch her cheek and she grabs me quickly and kisses me hard on my mouth holding the back of my head with her hand and just as quickly pulls away from me and sits quietly. She's shy again. For a moment she wasn't shy. I guess that's how it was when she started the fire and killed her parents, she lost her shyness for a moment. Now she's looking to see what I'll say. I look to the walls and fences covering the windows. It would be so easy to run away from here. "I think it's OK," I tell her, and I do. People have done worse things than kill their parents and I'm inclined to believe they deserved it because I think Tanya is nice. I don't think Tanya would have killed her parents if they didn't deserve it.

"Am I your girlfriend?"

I shrug my shoulders and the teacher walks back into the class-room with a thick book trapped under the arm of his tweed jacket.

Friday night is taco night at Reed. They're full of beef and good food from the outside. Not like the food we have here, frozen grape-fruit juice with spiders stuck inside or rotten meatloaf. And on Friday we eat the tacos in the rec room, not the lunchroom where the ceiling is covered in butter patties we've slapped onto the roof. Who needs butter?

Not everybody can have a taco. Only if we have money, if our parents or some friend from somewhere left some in our account. Most people can scrounge the three bucks from somewhere. Mr. Macy buys mine on a bet we had that nobody knows about. I eat my taco at a table with Jay, Mike, and French Fry.

"You still seeing that nigger?" Jay asks, brandishing a plastic knife in my direction, cutting the air by my chin.

"You fuck a nigger you'll have kids with six legs," Mike says. French Fry doesn't say anything. I take a big bite off my taco so my mouth is full and I don't have to respond.

"We're just teasing," Jay tells me. Across from us a table of inmates including the kid that smacked Mike with a pool cue is giving us dirty looks.

"It doesn't mean anything," I say but it does mean something. These morons are just too dumb to get it.

"I fingered the Indian girl in the closet by the gym," French Fry says now. Nobody cares. "I could never get girls on the outside. In here they're all sluts." And he laughs.

I spit my food into a napkin, stand up, and throw it in the brown, half-sized trashcan by the staff's office. Walk back to the table, over an outstretched leg, stretched to trip me. I hear laughing. A plastic fork flies over my left shoulder. I ignore it and sit back down. "We're gonna have trouble soon," Jay says. "We better stick together."

I nod, I know.

"Godless place," French Fry mutters into his food and I take a slug off my coke. There's going to be trouble rumbling on the floors of this place. Always is. I look at my half-eaten taco, the light yellow shell and deep brown filling, the thin trail of yellow grease seeping into the aluminum paper, and think about the shit on the walls in the east corridor.

Mike writes something on a sheet of paper. "Don't, Mike," I say.

"Shut up, nigger lover." He holds his sign up over his head in front of me and I feel the eyes from the next table burn into my shoulder blades then he puts the sign down on the table between all of us. It just says 'nigger.' What a word.

"We're not in jail," Jay says to me. "We're just crazy."

I crook half a smile, "They're crazy on the outside too."

"Crazy everywhere," French Fry chimes in.

"Yeah," Mike says underneath his flaming red hair, his voice rising, his freckles popping off his face. "Fucking crazy!" Staff looks out of the glass office. Mike stands up, "Crazy everywhere! Fucking crazy!" And now he's screaming and staff is pouring out into the rec room like oil in a pan and Mike howls, "C'mon motherfuckers!" and then he is tackled by this mass of five-dollar-an-hour authority in white shirts. I see Mr. Macy in the pile somewhere, silently shaking his head in the melee. A needle sticks Mike's leg. They tie him up and drag him down the hall. We know where he's going. They're going to chain him to a table for twelve hours. It's no way to live.

Jay nods in approval but I've never seen Jay lose his cool. A plastic fork lands in the middle of our table and there is laughing behind me. "Shit's going to go down," Jay says again.

"The apocalypse. The end of the world. Good versus evil," French Fry says.

"No," I correct them both. "A couple of idiots versus another couple of idiots with nothing to win but loads of time to kill."

"Take it easy," Jay says to me. "This is no time to be getting weird." I raise my eyebrow and Jay leans back like he's just smoked a cigarette. Fine. More laughing, more hallways, more drab colors and cheap plastic. It can't mean anything.

That night I think I hear Mike pulling at his chains, the long nylon cords strapping him to an eight-by-four wooden table like the kind people eat dinner at or have a barbecue on the beach with. I lie in my bed, feeling for my legs, concentrating on my stomach. Please let me get through it, please. Let me get through to morning with no demons. I lift my leg, it's a good sign, I can move. Please.

I look into the ceiling and for a moment it is burning. Searing shades of orange and yellow. Then it stops. I breathe in as deep as I can, pull the air filled with disinfectant and shit into my lungs. The air is thick, the walls rumble. I lift my other leg. I'm going to be OK tonight. I'm going to sleep tonight. I think I'm getting better. I can remember when I was younger and I would sit in bed and think. I would make up stories, or I would wonder why my father had called me an asshole, or why my mother had to piss in a bucket. "What kind of a solution is that?" I would think. A bucket by the couch. There had to be a better way, but I couldn't think of one. Everyday I would empty the bucket for her into the toilet, with all its urine and soaked tissue paper. Then I'd rinse the bucket and bring it back to her. She was always crying. But I was OK then. I could lie in bed and think, or read. I was unhappy as a child but I could move. Not like the depression I have now sometimes where I am a statue, a mummy. Where my legs stick to the bed like plaster. But I'm getting better, I can tell. My clouds are lifting.

Now I wonder what a life I can have. If I can be better, then I can do anything. I can go to the University of Chicago. I can study philosophy. Tomorrow I see Molly. I will tell her I am better and that I want to go back into the world.

Molly squints and takes me to her office. I ask her about the results of the test they gave me. "Am I depressed?" She squints again. "What am I paying you for?" and we both laugh a little.

"We'll go over those tests as soon as I can get a psychiatrist in to talk it over."

"But I want to know the results."

"I know you do." She crosses her legs now. She's killing me. I can't fathom her. Can't fathom what she thinks about there. I look at the top button on her shirt, then over her breasts.

"I love you," I whisper.

"What?" she asks.

I shake my head, look away. It's too much. How many more meetings with her before they let me out? And where do they intend to put me? I don't have any information. I scratch back by my neck and roll my head on my shoulders. "When can I get out?" I ask.

"And go where?" she squints. Does she think I have the answer to this question? It's impossible.

"Do you know where you'll be in twenty years?" I ask her.

"Don't be funny, Paul."

"Neither do I." I breathe heavy out of my nose. I wish I didn't have such bad skin. "I can't sit in here forever."

"Are you talking about running away?" This is a trap. I shake my head. "Because I would be very disappointed if you left. If you ran away. We need to get to a point where you can face things. You can't run away forever." She crosses, uncrosses, recrosses her legs.

"Some things aren't worth facing," I say to the wall. Can't look her in the eyes now. "Some things it's better to run away from." I think of my father handcuffing me to that pipe in the basement and trying to decide whether to pull down the pipe or to wait for him to come back and let me go. I made the wrong decision then. I waited for him to come back and when he came back, he let me go. But I knew, walking away from the yellow stucco house, I should have pulled down the pipe.

"Your father's sick," she says.

"You're telling me."

"No. He's really sick."

"I know, he's really sick. Sickest man I ever met."

"You're not listening Paul. I got a letter from your stepmother. His spine collapsed. He's in a wheelchair."

"Good."

"And he wants to see you." I shrug my shoulders. Why would I want to see him? I look at Molly's fingers. She doesn't wear any rings. Maybe they make her take them off before she comes in. Molly leans in close to me, puts her hand over my hand. I feel cold and when she takes me back to the ward she leaves the door open, an invitation, a birthday card, she leaves the door open so I can watch her switch, so I can watch her as she walks away. She's strong. She's powerful.

All of a sudden, my life is covered with women, like a thin blanket, like the blankets they give us in the ward, like the bed sheets we use in place of towels because we don't have any towels; we've never had any towels. We meet the girls tonight in the gym. It's an activity. We are in the gym playing basketball and most of us sit on the bleachers. It's an old gym. Two staff stand by each exit door, arms folded over their chests. One kid is over in the corner with a helmet on slowly banging his head against the wall. Nobody moves to stop him.

Tanya knows to meet me inside the bleachers where they can't see us, down under the wooden benches. No one cares. There are too many kids here, it's anarchy. Some kids are lifting weights with old universal machines, punching the air with fifty pounds on their arm. Others are hiding. I can see that many are hiding. I am hiding in my skin out in the open.

Tanya kisses me deeply on the mat. I have her pinned underneath me, her body, her shirt up, her breasts against my T-shirt. I kiss her and rub my hands over her, in her armpits. She doesn't smell good but I can forgive her for that the way she forgives me for being ugly. "When can we go," she asks, she begs. She thinks there is somewhere else. Somewhere outside.

"Soon," I lie. I can't do anything else and I kiss her, it seems like the right thing to do. And as I kiss her, as I taste the inside of her mouth, feel her nose against my nose, her skin against my bad skin, as I rub my hand under her, between her ass and the mat, as I do that I feel a deep pain like a bolt of lightning up my side, pushing me off of Tanya.

I look up. Tanya is at my side, and between the metal lines running under the bleachers and the sound of the basketball bouncing on the court and the chains running in the machines stands George and five other black guys. I stay seated, I'm at the lower end of the bleachers and I can't stand up. I feel my side where George kicked me and I think about screaming for Jay and Mike but I don't.

"What you doing with one of our bitches?"

I shrug my shoulders. "I don't know. Who cares?" He kicks me in the face and I go back and soon there are many feet on me and some scuffling, a dull scuffling sound in all the pain, which ends and fades to black.

I sit on the bed with Mike and Jay and French Fry lined up like three monkeys in a row on the creaky springs. I taste the blood still in my mouth, my eye swollen and black. I tap my foot. I'm waiting for Mike or Jay to say we have to go get them. We have to get them for doing this to me. They can't get away with it. Instead Jay says to me, "Told you not to get with no black chicks."

"What were you thinking?" Mike echoes. I look at him, freshly released, acting calm, pretending to be reasonable when really just a few hours ago he was tied to a table foaming at the mouth. And I know that when the apocalypse comes and they are burning and the hour is upon them I am going to walk over them. I will walk past them when they need me and not look back. Just go. When they stretch out their arms from the mud, as they are sinking, and waiting, praying for a rope from me, I will look away.

"So many walls in this place," I say. A deep moaning comes from the hall, a wailing, "I'm going to hell."

"Good, you fucking retard," Jay answers to the hallway.

"I'm going to hell," it says again.

"This can't be right. Huh?" I say, to break the monotony. To make some conversation. Nobody has anything to say tonight, just me with my swollen face and bag full of problems. A waste. Just a fucking waste.

Mike rubs the red marks on his wrists. "Gonna kill them one day," he mutters. Not long until he gets strapped to the table again. Crazy fucker. I want to tell him and Jay that I'm mad. They should defend me; they're not acting like family, like someone you should have loyalty to. It's one thing to be crazy, another to abandon your friends.

"I wouldn't care if you fucked a dog," I say, scratching my head. "And she's not a dog. Nothing wrong with her." Mike laughs, then Jay, then French Fry. "I'll bust your head," I say looking down at my hands, my fingernails bitten down to the skin and even below my fingernails, the skin peeling off straight to my knuckles. I'm talking to all of them and none of them but it doesn't matter because I don't look at them, I just play with my fingers, my big, ugly hands.

Molly touches my eye and I wince away from her like an animal exposed to light for the first time in weeks. She runs her finger over my cheek, I open my mouth a little expecting her to put her finger in my mouth, to suck on it like a baby bottle if she did. "C'mon," she says standing up, "we're going out."

I pile into her car, faces staring from the window. "Who's leaving?" the faces are asking. A blue Honda with a hatchback, a happy face dangling from the mirror. The car smells of pine and the sun washes over us. We drive through the grounds, Molly unbuttons the top of her shirt and rolls down the window a little and the breeze blows her hair and she turns to me, Molly who is thirty or more and I'm four-teen, Molly turns to me, her face full of light.

It seems to take hours to get off the grounds, the green lawns, the broken-down buildings. Reed is sparse, empty, under-populated. Really, nobody lives in Reed, since the ones that do live here don't exist and nobody knows their names. As we come out I look in the mirror and the buildings start to fade. Nothing's real.

Molly's car passes through the gate easily, the guard gives her a nod. I guess he's seen her car plenty of times, and then I start to wonder about her car, about who's seen it and who's been in it. Molly's car is a stick shift and she drives it with her legs slightly spread, her light brown skirt falling gently between them, waiting for my hand.

Back in civilization, the cars crowd the street, people walk their dogs, mumbling to themselves. They don't know how close they are. We don't go far, just to a Pizza Hut, weeds growing in the cement parking lot. Molly pulls the clutch, the car slows to a stop in front of this bright red disaster. She looks over at me, I wait for her kiss, for her lips, but I know that's just television. Her hand goes down, and unbuckles my seatbelt, then her own. We pause, our doors open, I step outside into the graveled light, the asphalt plain.

We take a booth in the back. Molly leaves her sunglasses on. Our feet touch under the table. "Back to civilization," she says. I don't know how to respond. I wish I also had a pair of sunglasses. A chubby waitress with bad skin and a headband takes our order and Molly orders a pizza for us, and a salad. "I thought you needed a break."

"Breaks are good," I say.

"Paul," her foot slides up my foot. "The court has issued an injunction. The state has taken custody of you." I wait for her to go on. I wonder what time it is, what day. They're blending. Where was I when the court was talking about me? Maybe I didn't exist in those moments. "I've decided to apply for a foster license, so when you are discharged you can stay with me." The car, it doesn't make sense. Where are the motives? Where are the others? Who else has been in her car? Are they lost in her eyes, her deep blue eyes drowning all of the boys she has taken home. She stretches her hand over the table, over my hand. TV? Her foot slides up the back of my leg, slightly, imperceptible. "I've never done this before, Paul. This'll be new for both of us."

Back at the ward I don't have to be searched since I've been with Molly, older, her blond hair. They don't have to search me; they know where I've been.

"Where've you been?" Mike wants to know.

"Molly."

"That's my woman."

"That's not your woman. That's your therapist."

"So."

"Look Mike. I can't help it. I'm required to meet with her once a week. What do you want me to do?" I spy the tables. Mike walks off down the hall. There is nothing here. Most everybody is just outside the main room at the pool table. The two TVs are going, up on metal racks, blasting us with information. I check the nurse's station. Mr. Macy is not in. This place is so small. I'm trying to go for a walk, to think. I can't think. I walk each end of the ward, the sides splitting off like wings from the rec room: a small room on either side of the nurse's station, and the bedrooms. It's a very small area. The two wings split from the nurse's station and dead end at thick steel bolted doors. Bright blue locked pools. I feel cramped; I bite my nails. A wave of something rises in my stomach and I pull it back. I'm getting better. I don't need to be here, not anymore.

Jay sits at a couch in the corner, arms outstretched. "Have a good lunch?" he asks.

"What are you talking about?"

"How was your pizza?"

"Couldn't keep it down. Threw up in the bathroom. How do you know about my pizza?"

"I know these things," he says, opening his mouth, flicking a small, pointy tongue. "There's trouble coming, Paul."

"I've had my trouble already," and feel the swell around my eye, the sharp pain in my ribs.

"That was nothing. There's real trouble."

"I'll be fine," I say.

"None of us will." I sit down next to him. He puts his hand in my stubbly hair, presses his fingers into my scalp. "You think you'll get out of here. Fly away, Paul." I let him keep his hand in my hair, he twists the ends in his fingers. "There is no outside, Paul. You can't get away from here. Where would you go? The rest of your life will always be this tiny compound, this tiny little hell. You must have done something really bad. You must have done something so terrible that the world shut its eyes to your pain." I hear the breath coming through his nose as he speaks. I try to stand up but his other hand grabs my shirt. "What did you do, Paul?"

"Let me go,"

Jay grabs tighter. "What'd you do?"

I struggle away from him, grab his wrist. "Or maybe you're just crazy," I say. His fingers slide away from my head, his long fingers. I want to cry now. I stand up and walk away, Jay's eyes burning me. I walk away, down the short hall. I fight back what's in my stomach. I don't have to cry, I'm trying to get better.

It's been raining for three days and I wonder when it will stop. Yesterday it was raining so hard they wouldn't let us go to school. They worried about the rain as cover. They worried about us hiding in the raindrops, ducking between the water, escaping through the fence. They're afraid they won't see us on the lawn, by the buildings, the black winding road, the forsaken basketball court overrun with weeds, the back wards.

I've been reading. I've been sitting on my bed watching the rain. First I was reading *Johnny Got His Gun*, but they took it away from me. They said it was inappropriate. I started reading the Bible but I found it dry, hard to read, and harder to believe. French Fry spends an hour with the Bible everyday. French Fry's crazy. Jay thinks the Bible's silly. Says he only gives respect to people who earn it first. So I've been reading *Les Misérables*, which Mr. Macy brought me. It's abridged but still runs over eight hundred pages. A lady on staff laughed at me once, told me I was just holding the book open, couldn't understand it. I told her I was smart for my age, could understand it just fine, and asked if she had read it and then laughed at her because I knew she hadn't.

Mr. Macy stands in my doorway. He has a few whiskers on his chin and pulls on them thoughtfully.

"Your father's here."

"Damn." I put down my book. "Only two hundred more pages." I hope this will impress him. I want to impress him. He smiles a bit. "What should I do?"

"You should probably see him," he tells me. "You don't have to, nobody can make you. But you'd be denying yourself information." I grab the book and follow Mr. Macy.

"Mr. Macy, why do you walk like a pimp?"

"Now how would you know what a pimp walks like?"

"I watch television. What else am I gonna do here."

"You better keep reading those books," he says pointing to the book in my hand. "That TV is gonna make you crazy for real." He laughs a little bit and stops at the door and nods to me. I go inside.

He's a monster. My stepmother sits, hands in her lap, gaunt, austere like a painting. Her pants neatly pressed tuck between her legs, her blouse rolls over her chest. My father's cheeks slide off his face, his large hands grip the handles of a second-hand wheelchair. Mother's? His head stabilized and bolted in by a network of metal rods holding his spine up. Wearing baggy corduroy, unshaven, big blue eyes full of anger and shame.

"Hello Paul," my stepmother says without moving, without even squirming an inch on that rotten chair. I look back to my father. A monster, Frankenstein, a machine. I can't decide whether to laugh or to cry, and do neither. I sit across from them, a low round table separating us. I want to run. Mr. Macy told me the other day that running is pointless. That I would find that out. That one day I'd run so far I'd find myself back in the same place, but older. Then I'd see.

"My boy. My beautiful boy." My father talks through his whiskers, chewing on his words. I can't not look at the metal bars on either side of his face, his large nose. "We want you to come home, son. We'll start a clean slate."

"But you shaved my head."

"I gave you a haircut."

"You beat me up."

"I used the necessary force to make the arrest."

"But I was sleeping." In the doorway it looks like Mr. Macy's body is shaking. Maybe he is laughing. We're quiet, and minutes pass. "I don't even know where you live."

"We'll take you there."

"Why don't you just write down the address and maybe I'll meet you?" More silence.

"You're my son," my father says, voice starting to rise, cheeks sliding off his face. He tries to pound his palms on the arms of his wheelchair but gets just a small thud.

"Look at you," I say.

More silence, more silence. Silhouettes and shadows. My step-mother finally shifts; I was waiting for her to. Nobody can sit in that position for that long without blinking. Ten days in the desert. No water, no companionship. She shifts a little more. "Your father needs your help, Paul." I shrug my shoulders. She pulls some files out of a briefcase hidden by the side of the chair. Mr. Macy pokes his head in the doorway, craning his neck around without moving his body, and goes back to standing. "We thought you might want to see these."

I know what they are immediately. They're Molly's files; they're thick. They have my test results, psychiatric recommendations.

"How'd you get these?"

"Your therapist sends them to us every week."

I nod, squeeze the manila envelope in my hand then push down on the plastic chair. "Well. I've got some reading to do. Thanks for the visit." I stand up, walk over by my father's chair. He looks up at me through his metal halo and I think of all the things I could do. Mr. Macy is looking in the room again. I kick the wheel of my father's chair and walk away.

• • •

"Why don't you take that dress off?" I mumble. Curled up, I'm a baby. I'm trying to be better; I take my thumb out of my mouth, roll onto my back. I peruse the papers that my father's read. I pull slightly on the sheets, not enough to pull them apart.

I place a chair on my bed, palms against the wall. Remove the ceiling slat for our secret hiding place, balanced precariously on the mattress. I take out a cigarette, two matches. Climbing down, I put the chair back, strike the match on the mirror.

The smoke is glorious. Haven't smoked in weeks. I go back to the pages. They say I'm depressed, I know I'm depressed. They estimate my IQ at 117. Prick bastards. I estimate their IQ at negative. I read on, pages and pages. Questions and answers. They think I'm lying. I've been lying all along. My father underlined that in red. They want to reunite me with my father. Here's Molly's application for temporary custody. It doesn't jibe. Doesn't ring. I scour the ceiling for a place to hang myself then close my eyes and let it pass away. "Things will get better," I tell myself. I think of how it will be when I'm older. I'll be beautiful, for a while. I'll be golden. My skin will clear up and I'll grow my hair long. I'll be so damn healthy. I'll forgive everyone. I'll forgive my father. What the hell. I'll date a beautiful therapist and she'll listen to everything I have to say, seven days a week. And I'll get my hands between her legs. I'll taste her.

Wish I had some music. I flick my ashes on the floor. A colorless floor, colorless windows. This file, this thick file which Molly didn't want me to read but she sent to my father the monster every week. Colorless also. I smoke the last and spit on the cigarette and put it out in the papers and casually discard them in the green metal bin by the office, in front of the rec room, where all the social workers and a smattering of security guards are standing around Jay who lies on the floor bleeding from the head.

The halls seem white today: stark, dirty and glowing. I don't know what happened to Jay and I feel sure I never will. This is what I saw, or I think I saw: Jay's face, like a skull with skin pulled tight over it, blood by his ear, his eyes open, stringy long blond hair around his head like a halo. The guards and the staff moved around him slowly, talked slowly. I would like coffee. We never have caffeine here. The sounds slowed, the molecules in the air became thick, and surprisingly comfortable.

I stood in the entrance but was told to go, go away. "Go where?" I asked and looked to the locked door at the end of the hall and thought, "Alarms go off all the time." I made one quick motion towards the alarm and then turned and walked slowly back to my room and laid on the molecules, on my bed with my hands behind my head and stayed that way until morning.

Now the hallways are dirty. I didn't go to school today. I'm sitting on a bright red couch, waiting for Molly to spread open the two large doors that lead down the halls to the offices. I'm waiting to smell Molly and the open doors, her skirt, her shoes. I'm twitching; I itch.

The doors open. Molly stands, the lamps from the hallway back-light her golden hair. She squints. Her blouse hangs off her arms in rolling waves. A light green blouse, she's wearing a ring, and there's a breeze behind her. From where?

We walk the halls. She squints and smiles at me while I keep my hands in my pockets. The halls run by, the slatted ceiling. We pass a room I've never seen before. A long room and a man sits there at the end of a table in a tan suit with a large head and his hands folded over each other. He looks like he's talking to someone but no one is there. He thinks his suit is enough; it's not. "It's not," I say out loud, but gently.

"What did you say?" Molly asks, turning to me. I'm watching her ankles. She sees me staring at her calves, her creamy white stockings. "You must be fascinated." And she turns back.

She's been cleaning her office. I step in ahead of her, sit down, and cover my face with my hands. The books have been put away. The papers sit in white boxes by the radiator. Molly sits down, squinting. "So your father gave you some papers…"

"It's true, Molly." I rub my fingers on my face, over my nose. I'm looking through fingers. I stop, pull my hands away, stroke my hair forward. Months later there's still nothing there. My hair's not growing back. Maybe I have cancer. "Am I dying?" She looks at me quizzically. I drop my hands to my lap and look down at the floor. "You shouldn't have given him those papers…when you wouldn't give them to me."

"Should I not have given them to him because I hadn't let you read them, or because he shouldn't have them?" She crosses her legs. I see her do it. I see ever so slightly she pulls her skirt back an inch with her pinkies so I can see her thighs.

I can't think for a second. Can't understand what she's saying. I turn to the window; the outside is there, calling me. Calling me to the grass or the pavement. I can't think. Finally, finally, finally. "It doesn't matter," I say. "You shouldn't have. It was wrong. And you know it was wrong and you know why."

"Oh." She wasn't ready for that from me. But it's a hit. She uncrosses her legs, smoothes her skirt, breathes for a minute. Stops. I stop with her and then she smiles at me, and her legs uncrossed she starts to raise her skirt again. "What do you want, Paul?"

I watch her uncovered knees. I want her smell. I want to crawl inside her. "I want to be beautiful. Just for a moment. I've never known anything except ugly."

She laughs, short and soft. "You are beautiful." She stands, comes. Her fingers on my cheek. I pull away. She's kneeling with me, I'm afraid of her. She touches my leg and her hand runs the outside of my thigh. She goes back to her seat. So close, but still, out of touching range. Does she want me to rape her? Is she aware of anything? Who's messed up here? Because I'm feeling pretty sane.

"It's just…"

"Yes?" She leans forward.

I tell her. "I've never had a girl." She nods. "So I've never been betrayed which I guess is part of a relationship. And when you don't have relationships you don't have to worry…about these things."

"Do you feel I betrayed you, Paul?"

"Absolutely. You definitely betrayed me. You used me." We pause. I lean back in the chair, exhale, but continue, to the walls, to Molly, to everyone who might want to hear which maybe is no one. "We sit in this office, month after month. You go home and I go back to the ward. You know what they call it? B East. We call it Beast. Have you seen the shit on the walls? There is human shit on the walls. Look at these pants. There're holes in them. You never even got me a pair of pants." I laugh and I rub my naked knee. "What exactly is it that you're supposed to do for me if you can't even get me a pair of pants?" She's not listening now. She's on automatic waiting for me to finish. She learned that in therapist school. I stop. Catch my breath. It's more than I usually say. I can hear the world outside her windows. I stand and Molly stands with me. "I want to thank you, Molly. I want to thank you for everything." She nods; she's absent.

"I'll see you next week, Paul," she says. The squint returning to her features. "We'll talk some more. You're going to be getting out soon."

• • •

"Your eye looks better," Tanya whispers in class. My eye has been healing. There's only a gray shadow around it. Maybe I should just paint it black so people will stop hitting me there. It seems to be an unlucky eye.

I place my hand on her leg under the table. The teacher looks up from his book then back. The students lounge by the windows, or drool in the corners. This is the smart class. Mike and French Fry are just down the hall in the less-than-smart class. I feel that in this room, only Tanya and I exist. The rest is wallpaper. "I'm going to take care of you," I whisper into her ear.

She scribbles on the sheet of paper in front of her, "I know you can." Most of us will do what we have to do to save ourselves. After that there's only suicide. Staying in Reed would be suicide for me. Not today or tomorrow, but soon enough. Maybe on Molly's kitchen floor. I picture her house, a small bungalow, well kept with clear glass. A thick, comfortable bed. And I just know if I ever saw it I would kill myself immediately. I think not killing myself is victory enough.

Reed has a fourteen-day discharge policy. If you run away and don't get caught for fourteen days you are officially released and they stop looking for you. Basically, if you can stay away for fourteen days you must not be crazy.

Our escape is fairly simple. I have twenty dollars that Mr. Macy gave me a while ago and told me to keep it in my shoe because I was going to want it. Between classes, instead of going to the bathrooms or the closets, we walk straight out the door. We run away from the road and over through the grass. We're holding hands and Tanya stops for a second to look in a square brick bunker with a broken window and poles rising floor to ceiling, twenty of them at least, the paint chipped away and rusted. I pull and she runs again. There is nobody. We are away from the road; nobody comes here. We are in the back wards and we can hear the ghosts. After fifteen minutes we come to a fence. We climb and help each other over and we're on Irving Park Road and the cars are going past. A big green bus pulls up and we climb on and pay the fare. We look back at the fence and it looks like any fence for any person's backyard or garden. No one would ever know what's back there. It looks like a garden.

Tanya gives my hand a squeeze. We sit on Day-Glo orange seats with no idea where we're going but I think a strong sense that things will be OK, if just for a while, though nobody can tell these things.

"Where are we taking this bus to?" she asks. Sometimes cars pass the bus, other times the bus cruises along just fine.

"The end of the line," I say in reply, and she wraps her arms around me and lays her head in my lap. I run my fingers over her cheek and we wait and see what happens next. We wait and see what the world will bring.

2. TOOLSHED PARADISE

Initially the sun and boxtops suffice, a perfect world for a little while. One nice day we hide by the exit of a large red theater and as the people are leaving we go in and this way we are able to see Superman III. After the movie Tanya says, "That's a pretty good idea. Let's take a halfpenny from everybody. Then we'll be millionaires."

"First we'll need an office."

"And a computer. You can get that can't you."

"Tanya, I'll get you whatever you want."

She grips my arm. "Paul, you're a real man." My cheeks flush red.

Tanya and I sleep on a roof on top of a convenience store on the edge of Wicker Park. We climb over the bins and pipes along the back of the building to the top. On the roof we lie on the gravel, inside our cardboard shelter, and crawl as deep into each other as we can to stay warm. We set the boxtops up like a hut to protect us from the wind. We don't have sex but sometimes I touch her breasts and her thighs. The nights are cold everywhere. In the morning we crawl back down, trying to be quiet. We don't want the owners of the convenience store to know that we are sleeping on their roof.

Walking though an alley in the morning Tanya says, "Do you notice it's getting colder?"

"It's not so bad."

"But it's getting colder I mean."

We've been gone from Reed a couple of weeks now. Behind the Dominick's is a trash bin. I crawl inside to find things that have just been thrown away. I can tell because they will still be cold. We take milk and a packet of ham. In front of the deli fresh bread rolls have been delivered and wait by the door in paper bags for the deli to open. We grab a roll and make sandwiches.

Sitting on a bench after school hours we watch some kids play basketball in the park. A couple of them leave and the remaining kids ask us if we will play with them. They need two more players to make four on four. I say, "OK," and Tanya touches my hand. Tanya and I are on separate teams and we run up and down the court with the other kids dribbling the ball and passing it back and forth. The court is half sized. We play for a while and then the kids that had left come back. They dump crowbars and sawed off golf clubs onto the grass. We keep playing but I notice the tall kid with the crew cut red hair watching us. I guard Tanya and while I am watching the kid who is watching us Tanya drives past me and scores a basket.

"What the hell was that," one of my teammates asks me.

"I guess I wasn't paying attention."

He grabs the ball and the game stops. "You weren't paying attention? Get the fuck out of here."

"Yeah, get the fuck out of here," the tall red-headed kid says and throws a rock at me. "We don't need you here anymore."

"Take it easy," I tell them. "We were just going to ask you if you wanted to get back in."

"Get the fuck out of here," another one says and steps forward and punches me in the face. I stop, walking away won't help now. I feel my cheek swell. Tanya grabs my hand hard. "What?" the boy asks. "Are you two married? What?"

"Yeah. We're married." Tanya and I walk away from the park. At the corner we stop at the water fountain and we can still hear the ball bouncing on the court.

We wander north after that, up Kimball, through Jefferson Park and into Edgewater. We become urban nomads, wandering the city. We taste the Chicago neighborhoods, rich, each with its own sounds and smells. We find our food in dumpsters and in quarters gleaned from the streets. We sleep in doorways, alcoves, and under a bridge at the canal. Our faces covered in dirt. I stay up at the canal because I am afraid of rats and I can hear them poking their filthy noses into the water's murky pools. We see other homeless men and women pushing shopping carts down Wilson Avenue. We see them in alleys, squeezed in the narrow passage between garages, sheltered against the walls of large industrial buildings. We know that most of them, hundreds and thousands, lie huddled on discarded mattresses on Lower Wacker Drive in the loading docks of downtown Chicago. We avoid other homeless people. We don't want to know them.

Then the rains come. Everything we do centers around getting away from the rain. We break into a boiler room but the pipes keep banging, making us think someone is coming. We don't want to meet people. We stay up all night in a laundromat. We have to get out of the rain.

Tanya's hand is soft and warm but the world is stacked up against us. The cold rain keeps falling and has thickened the grass that covers the yards and the parks. Night has fallen and we step across a yard of someone's house, silently pressing the latch on an old picket fence, silently moving across someone's sleeping property. In the back, behind a row of trees, I break the lock to a toolshed with a long steel bar and we crawl inside, soaking wet, and huddle together beneath the pitter pat of raindrops.

"This is not good," I say. We had not planned on this much rain. We had not thought through the weather.

"Our toolshed paradise," Tanya replies.

"We'll be OK here. Just for a night. Tomorrow we'll figure something out." I rub my hands on my pants, trying to get dry, but my jeans are soaked.

"OK. Let' not talk about it. Let's talk about something warm."

I laugh at her suggestion and she squeezes my hand. I start to shiver, just a little at first, but then more, and harder. I hate shivering from the cold. When the rain gets under my skin and stays there I start to shake. I feel Tanya start to shiver as well. The rain comes down harder, like the end of a symphony, strong, loud drum beats battering the wooden roof of the toolshed. "Fine. What do you want to be when you grow up?"

"Happy."

"Good answer."

"You?"

"Beautiful."

"If that's all you want then you can retire now."

"Don't say that," I tell her. "I'm not beautiful."

"To me."

"Good enough."

We sit and shiver and the rain provides the music and the rain coming from Tanya's hair and Tanya's lips fills the air. "Tanya," I say. "Tanya, Tanya. I love you." Tomorrow we will have to come up with something. Tomorrow something will go our way. I hug her.

"You love only me."

"I love only you."

I slip my hand inside her shirt and Tanya lets out a breath as the door to our toolshed paradise creaks inward from the pounding of the rain.

The morning's rays knock through the wooden slats and dust swims in the streaks of light. "Time to get up," she whispers. "The rain has stopped." The music gone and replaced with a soft wooden silence. "Up."

I sit and rub my eyes. The light pours through the slats and illuminates the rakes and shovels that line the walls of the toolshed. I stand and open the door slowly to peer against the wet lawn. Where did the rain go? The sun is blinding. All of the clouds are gone, a pale blue sky stretches through the treetops and the sun gleams across the wet lawn. Beyond the lawn sits a stately suburban house. No one moves across its living room. I wonder if we could break into the house and steal the food in the refrigerator. Whoever lives there has cash. The house is large, square with white columns. Like what I think my father's house looks like. Perhaps that is my father looking towards the toolshed from the kitchen. No, no one is there. No one is in that house. I felt it yesterday. I felt that this one would be safe. None of the lights were on in that house, that large house, not a single one. I just knew no one was there.

"You know, in the morning, we should be brushing our teeth."

"Look, I am," Tanya tells me. She slowly layers phony toothpaste on a make-believe toothbrush. Then she turns the faucet on an invisible sink and spends an elaborate two minutes brushing her teeth including gargling and spitting.

"It's like us," I say. Tanya arches her eyebrows. "We're living in a toolshed while the rest of the world lives in houses."

"Paul, the rest of the world does not live in fancy houses. We are closer to the rest of the world than the people that live in that house."

"Got a quarter?"

"Spare some change?"

"Got forty cents?"

Close to the mall we ask people for what they have in their pockets until we have enough and then we buy orange soda, french fries, and a sandwich at a hot dog stand.

"They're not looking for us anymore," Tanya says.

"Reed. Fourteen days." Our fourteen days is long up. We have been staffed out of Reed. We were never there. We have been erased. I don't know how long we have been gone now. More than twenty, thirty days. The days run together. The one thing that is clear as time passes is that the weather is turning colder. We are heading footlong into winter. "What are we going to do?"

Tanya knows what I am talking about. She knows about the winter.

"I have a cousin," she tells me. "But I am afraid to go to him because he will get in trouble."

"I don't have anybody."

"Don't feel sorry for yourself."

I turn my face away from her. I hate it when she corrects me. A man stumbles, drunk, through the door and asks for a hot dog. He turns his toothless grin on us. "What have we got here? A couple of kids having lunch? Your mamma give you money for lunch? Don't she know you're supposed to be in school?" He laughs at his own joke.

I look back towards Tanya. She chews on a french fry and sucks down her soda pop. I don't know why adults are always trying to make everything hard for us, acting like they know so much. Tanya is innocent, and should be protected from them. She is also strong. She protects me as well and she makes me stronger than I am.

"Mind if I sit with you fine young people and enjoy my sandwich?"

"Yeah, I mind," I tell him.

"What? You all having a meeting? You don't want to be interrupted. I suppose you're the chairman of the board and this here little girl is your secretary. Is that right? Are you his secretary?" He nudges her shoulder with his finger and she moves away from him.

"Hey buddy," the guy behind the counter calls. "Here's your sandwich. Get the fuck out of here."

"Oh, oh, OK. It's like that. I suppose you are the security guard." The man snatches the brown paper bag off the counter. "It's wonderful the way you be running shit around here, Mr. President. You be running shit just fine." He touches Tanya's face with his finger and grabs the door. I pick up my soda and throw it at him but the door closes and the paper cup splashes against the glass leaving a sticky orange explosion along the windows and floor. The man continues on laughing, laughing at the explosion from the other side of the glass.

Then the counter guy is in my face. "What the fuck is wrong with you? What the fuck did you do that for? I'm going to fucking kill you."

"Don't kill me."

"Don't kill him."

"What the fuck! Where the fuck are you two from? I want you out of here. Get the fuck out of here."

Tanya and I gather ourselves up and step out into the cold. I see down the street the drunken man weaving along the sidewalk. I see the train tracks up ahead and corner stores and shitty supermarkets and that fucking jerk that represents it all weaving along the sidewalk.

The cold comes to us. There is very little we can do. The streets are cold and the people walking them wear thick down jackets, leather jackets with scarves. We go into a Salvation Army Thrift Store and ask if we can have jackets.

"I'm sorry," the lady says. "This is a store."

"You're supposed to be helping people like us. That's the point, right?"

She looks skeptical and then she grabs two thick, ratty jackets off the hook with big furry hoods and I decide that The Salvation Army is a good place. We walk down to the lake and watch the big waves roll in on the deserted beaches. Soon the snows will come. We walk along to Montrose where people store their boats in the harbor. The boats sit there all winter. Nobody sails in the winter. The boats just sit and Tanya and I sit there in the wind watching the boats. We are just wind.

After a while I suggest we go to a church and Tanya says she doesn't mind but that churches scare her and she doesn't believe in anything anymore. I tell her that maybe somebody in a church will give us a blanket and they won't rat us out because nuns are sworn to secrecy.

The church sits on a corner by a train station and a used bookstore. It is the color of an old car, like rust and dirt. The church has long gray stairs and a sign proclaiming, "All Are Welcome," except the sign is missing an *e* so it actually says, "All Are Welcom." Inside, a nun in a black dress prays next to an altar. We stand in the space between the benches and when the nun is done praying she comes to us and invites us to sit with her in the church office. We sit and talk to the nun. She asks me where my parents are and I tell her my father is in some house in the suburbs. She asks Tanya where her parents are and Tanya does not answer.

"Look," I say. "We just wanted to see if you had some blankets we could borrow. We thought that because you are Catholic you might give us some blankets."

"A shrewd little businessman aren't you?" The nun smiles at me but it is not enough to make her pretty. "I'll tell you what. If you promise to come back tomorrow and talk with me some more I think I can find a couple of blankets for you. There are people that can help you. Good people. You don't need to be on the run."

"Will they separate us? Will they send us to different places?" Tanya asks.

"I don't know, darling. I don't see why they would."

"Because we're not married and they don't care about us."

"Yeah," I join in. "The State has a policy of family first. They don't care about us. They want to force us on relatives."

"You are a shrewd little businessman."

"Yeah. Well look, we are going to go. Are you going to give us some blankets?"

"Yes. Are you going to come back tomorrow."

"Maybe."

As the day closes Tanya and I make our way back across the city with our blankets swung over my shoulder. Now we are at our yard again. The one with the toolshed, our toolshed paradise. We sneak across the grass and into the tiny house with the rakes and the shovels hanging along the walls. I lay one blanket across the floor and we lie down and get under the other. Tanya hugs close to me.

We have needs. We need to find a way to eat. We need to find a place to shower. Our hair is bunched up in sticky knots. We have needs that we have to meet. I feel Tanya pressing into me as I stare into the darkness thinking about our needs and it occurs to me that Tanya doesn't think about our needs the same way. Tanya believes that if we stay together then we will be OK. She believes that we can sustain each other by giving energy back and forth but I don't believe that. Tanya is a romantic. I believe we need clothes and showers and heat and food and space. I am not a romantic. I do not think we can do it on our own.

"I don't want them to separate us. I'm not going back to talk with that nun. She wants to separate us. She doesn't want us to be together. She thinks we are living in sin. She hates us, the thought of us. I could tell it. I could see it. We're sinners." The rakes and the shovels nod their agreement with Tanya.

I kiss Tanya for her different needs and the world and I promise that we will stay together. It's simple.

I stand in the grass while Tanya sleeps. She didn't notice as I disentangled myself from her arms. I stand in the grass and I see the movements in the house. The house stands there on the other side of the trees. The house that owns this toolshed. We just want a little piece. If they would just give us this tiny little piece of what they have then we could be happy. We could get more blankets and stay warmer. Just this little space, this toolshed. Or if they would just give us a piece of their well manicured green lawn, then we could build our own toolshed.

I see the movements in the house. Black shapes moving through the rooms. I am behind the trees, hidden by shadow. They should not be able to see me here but I feel the stares from the house and I think to myself that they should just give us this tiny piece of what they have and they should leave us alone. They should not touch Tanya's face with their fingers. Tanya worries about them. Doesn't trust them. They have lied to us both. A separate nation, a toolshed nation, that would be just fine.

I lie back next to Tanya. "I can't sleep when you are gone," she whispers to me and lays an arm across my chest. I stare up at the dusty wood and the tools hanging along the walls.

"It's good to be wanted," I whisper back but I am thinking of our needs and I'm trying to figure out how to meet those needs. The needs that are mounting up one on top of another. We're getting buried under them. We smell bad. Our skin is thick with dirt. Our needs are mounting and the winter is taking hold. "I want to go back to the church," I tell Tanya. "Let's just go back and shower and stuff. Let's get clean."

"I don't want to be clean. I don't want to go there."

"Tanya, we have to shower. We're like animals."

"The city is wilderness," Tanya tells me.

The nun is happy to see us again. I ask her right away if we can shower and she says of course. Tanya showers first and the nun gives her clothes to change into when she is done. I sit with the nun and the nun asks me how I am feeling and I tell her I am feeling fine and she asks me if I miss my parents and I say no.

"You know," the nun starts. "Your parents probably miss you a lot. I am sure they would like to see you. If you wanted me to I would call them and set up a meeting between you."

"First off," I answer her back. "Don't be so sure that I am missed.

Second, I don't have their phone number. I don't even know where they live."

The nun frowns and we sit in silence for a while and then Tanya comes back in wearing old blue jeans that are too long and are tight in the thighs, a thick, baggy sweater that looks like it was made out of potato sacks. She looks ridiculous and unhappy. The nun remarks on how quick she was and Tanya gives her that same look again. The nun gives me a pair of jeans to change into and a sweater and leads me off.

The water in the shower is perfect. I let the warm water run over my body, carrying off the smell of being rained on and the places we have slept. An unmarked container holds industrial soap and I rub the soap all over and rinse off and then soap up again and again. I rub the soap in my hair. I don't notice the time passing. I stand under the shower, pulling the knots out of my hair but suddenly I realize it has been at least twenty minutes and Tanya will be getting upset so I step out of the shower and dry off and put on my new/used clothes and go back.

In the front room the nun is just putting down the phone and Tanya is gone. I hold the air for a moment from the doorway and run my eyes over the nun, over her feet, her long skirt, her shirt, her necklace, her face. "Where's Tanya?"

"She just went to use the bathroom."

I don't believe her now and I understand what Tanya saw yesterday. Her fingers are too close to the phone. I'm just slower to notice things but now I do. I notice the closet, the locked windows with deep brown paint. The phone next to her hand on the table is a dirty kind of tan, a filthy, cheap tan. It's ugly and cheap looking and her nails are close to the phone. Behind her Jesus is hanging on a cross smiling. I don't think I would smile if they hammered me into a cross. I don't think I would smile at all. I would be unhappy if they did that to me, if my own father sat and watched while the men and women of the town nailed me into stakes of wood, hurled rocks at me and called me names. I don't think that I could ever forgive my father for that. Then Tanya steps back in.

"Let's go," I say.

"OK," Tanya agrees.

"No wait. I want to talk to you two about some things."

"Not today. Tomorrow. There's plenty of time tomorrow." I grab Tanya.

"Wait."

"Tomorrow. We have a lot to do today. Today is very busy." We hurry out of the office and through the church with all of the stained glass and rows and rows of wooden pews. We hurry out the big wooden doors and down the steps past two men in gray suits walking inside.

"I won't go again," Tanya tells me and this time she really means it and I nod and we head down Broadway toward Wilson and into Uptown.

Uptown is populated with junkies and clinics and homeless and the services that support them. Uptown is downtown for the homeless. We look eagerly towards the grown men waiting in the chow line to get their food from the shelters. The shelters ID the men. They won't give food or beds to people that are underage, to runaways. We look at the scraggly old men with green beards, dying all of their alcoholic lives for this and we want what they have, a place in line.

"What happened to our youth, Tanya?"

"It's not over yet."

Roosevelt University is an enormous piece of black glass. Across from that a game room. Dealers hang out there passing fistfuls of tiny baggies into the hands of the buyers walking past. "See that game room?" I tell Tanya and point across the street to Dennis's Arcade and its multi-colored lights, half of them missing, shattered by kids with rocks.

"Yes."

"One time I was in there playing video games. I had bummed some quarters. I was homeless at the time, you know. Sleeping on this rooftop. I had been homeless for a while. I guess like we are now. And I'm playing video games and this old guy comes over and asks me if I want some more quarters. It was a guy I had already asked for a quarter and the first time he had said no. I had asked him right out front as I was going in. But there he was, offering me quarters, so I took them and played games. I really like video games, to tell you the truth. I'm pretty good at them too."

"I bet you are."

"Anyway, he hangs out and watches me play and then he asks me if I need a ride anywhere. I tell him I need to go to the South Side and he says he'll give me a ride as far as downtown and give me money for the subway."

"You believed him?"

"I was young. So the guy takes me over by Foster Beach. You know the part where the park kind of sticks out into the water and there are always all those cars there at night, by the golf course? Behind where the Spanish dudes play soccer?" Tanya nods her head. "And he parks the car and says he's not gay, but he'll give me ten dollars if I pull down my pants, just to see."

"Did you do it?"

"I thought about it. But then I said no and he said OK and drove me to the train station and gave me a dollar fifty."

"You should have done it."

"Yeah. I wish he was still around."

"I had a sister that was a prostitute," Tanya tells me.

"How'd she like it?"

"I don't know. She didn't talk about it much. I don't think she was very good at it. She never had any money. And then one day she was gone and never came back."

"That's too bad."

"I didn't care. She ignored me all the time anyway."

A flake of snow falls on my nose. Then another. I look at Tanya. A few white flakes have already landed in her hair. "Oh no." I watch as her hair becomes white and she ages in front of me, and the street and the buildings become white and age in front of us as well. The white snow falls in the darkest wrinkles in the lines on Tanya's face. We start to walk, then faster. The snow is coming. Not hard, but the snow is here. We were going to find something today but we didn't. We did not fulfill our needs. We stuff our hands in our pockets and tramp across the city. We are over three miles away from the toolshed we broke into. I don't want to go there again. I saw the faces this morning.

"Forget the toolshed," I tell Tanya. "Let's see if we can't break into a boiler room."

"We don't have time, Paul. We've run out of time. We have to go to the toolshed tonight. Tomorrow we'll find another place." She has grown old with white snow in the time it took us to run out of time.

"Fuck, Tanya."

She presses her hand to her mouth and then we start to walk as fast as we can. "Tomorrow," she says. "I'll sign up for classes, or you should. Tomorrow we'll make a plan. Maybe we could get a ride down south where it's warm. There's no law that says we have to stay in Chicago. Oh, Paul. Paul."

When we arrive we lie under our blanket, on top of the other, the snow begins to melt in our hair and in our clothes and then we are just wet. We lie in the dark shed and I hear the rumblings and the whispers from the rakes and the shovels. The rakes and the shovels do not approve, and the snow hits the roof making light sounds of coming apart. Tanya touches my side, touches my cheeks on my face. All I've ever wanted is to be touched the way Tanya touches me. Tanya takes off my shirt and kisses me. Kisses my chest.

"Tanya, I'm cold."

"Breathe," she tells me. "Breathe, baby, breathe."

I lay still and try to focus on her lips and not the cold. I realize now, truly in this moment, something about Tanya. I realize it but I can't put words to it. I won't put words to it. But I realize it right now. We are not pretty. We are two ugly homeless kids trying to relax in a toolshed. But the moment is pretty. The moment is beautiful. I touch her side. She takes off her own shirt and she runs her breasts over my face. She touches the sides of my face with her hands. Her breasts are large and fade with the darkness. Her breasts are a feeling. And the feeling is her nipple poking between my teeth.

• • •

Things change. Emotions change. People fall in and out of love. People lie to each other in the subtlest of ways. When we make promises to each other we can't keep we are lying. When we say, "till death do us part," we are ignoring forces beyond our control, and we are lying to the people that matter most. That's what I think. But it is unavoidable. Lies are part of relationships. I have never known any-body that I have not lied to or has not lied to me.

People lie to each other. Things change. Life is full of meaningful disappointment and lucky chance. The police don't knock. The police just come in. We have been deluding ourselves, living in a toolshed. They grab Tanya while I stand in the doorway and stare across the stalks of grass covered in a fine frost, covered with ants and bugs all killed by the frost, all of the microscopic insects of the world dead beneath a thin layer of snow. I stand in the doorway, watch Tanya's body twisting and screaming in the air, a victim of the hands of the police and they pull her from the front and the back. A victim of an unkept promise.

While Tanya is screaming for her parents and the fire that con-sumed them, that took their lives, that took back only the tiniest piece of what they took from Tanya which was so much, which was so hor-rible a thousand fires could not burn it away, while Tanya is screaming I stare across the blades of grass and the intricate frost to the house with its white pillars. Faces are in the windows watching as the police wrestle Tanya out of the toolshed. The police didn't knock. They just came in and took what they wanted.

I move aside as they drag Tanya's twisting body through the door-frame and she screams. Her screams are mighty. They are taller than the trees that were supposed to hide us from the house across the grass. As she goes by I try to lock her eyes but I miss them. So instead I grab onto the arm of a police officer and he stops, they stop, and he looks at me for a moment. It's a brief moment. Two stopped police officers and Tanya squirming between them. The cop pointedly looks down at my fingers on his sleeve. I let go of his sleeve and they take my love away from me. When they push her into their car I can't hear her screaming anymore. And that's all there is.

I trudge across the yard and sit down on the front steps of the house. What matters now? A woman with gray hair comes out and asks me if I would like a hot chocolate. She is old with long, skinny legs, wears gray corduroys and a thick sweater. The world is reduced to shapes and colors. "OK," I tell her. She comes back with a tall gray mug filled with chocolate that she hands me. I sip on it thoughtfully.

The lady goes back into her house and closes the door. All I hear is, "click," and all I can think of is the end.

The snow has stopped. A strange sun has appeared above the buildings. An orange and bright but not warm sun. The sun alone cannot keep the runaways out of the boiler rooms or the rooftops of convenience stores. The sun cannot stop us from robbing houses or breaking into stores. The sun doesn't help at all. The sun only helps when it is in season. I am sitting on a porch with a cup of hot chocolate in my hand. I'll do what I can with it. I like hot chocolate. I always have.

3. ADLAI STEVENSON HOUSE

Whenever I am searching, I am searching for you. I look for you first in every crowd. Every image is a replacement, every doorway a path back home. When I am with you the world is quiet. I drown in you. I stare in people's faces searching for your eyes. I keep letters in a book that I mean to send to you when I find out where you are.

The grass is green and beautiful but covered in a thin layer of frost. I speak into a cup, the steam and the smell of chocolate rising over my face. It is early in the morning and the houses are all sleeping and the only sound is the sound of a car or two and a bird. An hour later they come back for me with their flashing blue lights. Surly police officers, a blue and white car, the logo near the taillights reads 'To Serve and Protect.' I dump the last of the chocolate into the bushes. I sit on the front steps of someone's house wearing a pair of black denim pants trying to sort out my day. The man takes me by the arm and pulls me towards the car and a sharp pain shoots through my shoulder and then he pushes me in the back door. These cars, with their dark blue seats and plastic floors, I've been in them plenty of times before.

They drive me down to the Robert Taylor Homes away from our toolshed. I look out of the window for Tanya along the Dan Ryan freeway and in the trains that speed by the meridian. I search the blur of faces. I look for her in the buildings and the girders and the passing cars. I knock on the grating separating me from the two men in the front seat. "Where is she?" I ask. The driver doesn't turn around and the other man stares at me with cold brown eyes, like he is going to kill me and bury me beneath the Dan Ryan freeway, under the trains and the buildings and Comiskey Park where I will never be found. I open my mouth and run my hand behind the seat. Sometimes there are drugs there, when the police don't pat somebody down, a last ditch effort to hide the evidence. As we drive the buildings break down. We come to a place where the people look away when they see the police car. We arrive on a broken street at a three-story brick compound that is drowned out by the immensity immediately behind it, the towering Robert Taylor Homes.

The Robert Taylor Homes are the largest housing projects in the world. They tower over the Dan Ryan freeway like broken teeth, with miles of chain-link fence casing in the outdoor stairwells. Black faces press against the fence; laundry hangs from it. Black stains mark the gray cement walls around the window frames. Their shadows fall across the abandoned North-South train tracks, own every unlit street light, swallow Garfield Park all the way to Sunset Church. They own State Street from 25th to 65th, forty blocks of anarchy with tens of thousands of tenants. Gym shoes hang from telephone lines like flags. Black and blue for Royals, black and red for Vice Lords, black and gold for Gaylords. The gym shoes blow back and forth in the wind on breezy days. The fortress liquor stores line up across from the Robert Taylor Homes; they are more common than fire hydrants, they sell plastic cups full of whiskey to grown men. The men shoot dice along the cracks in the sidewalk lit by the glow of trashcan fires. Dark lines in their faces crease in anticipation. Small bits of change float from the government's hands onto Robert Taylor's stairwells in the form of welfare, social security. The change is not enough. It falls through the fingers. The buildings crumble, the cement is layered with cracks. Along the Robert Taylor Homes like tufts of grass there are churches, small government buildings, outreach projects, schools and basketball courts with bent rims. State Street is four lanes of black tar. Occasionally an automobile lumbers its length. Otherwise, there are vacant lots with abandoned cars growing like bushes in the dirt and the rocks. The streets all dead-end, so unless you know your way it is nearly impossible to get out. Children sit on the guardrails and throw stones at rats. Grown men and women walk around in underclothes in the summer and blankets in the winter. The population laughs at bus stops, hides under dimming hallway lights. Many have gone mad with poverty. Hidden in the shadows of these enormous buildings, these concrete mountains, among post offices covered in barbed wire and the green glass of broken bottles, there are a smattering of group homes where the state hides the children when there is nowhere else to go.

They hide me in a tuft of grass called Adlai Stevenson House after a man that was almost president for boys that never will be. Stevenson House sits next to the Robert Taylor Homes like a mole on a person's face. Stevenson House holds the worst the system has to offer, the twelve-year-old murderers, now seventeen and freshly released. The kids who went to Juvi for something and their parents wouldn't pick them up. The heroin house rescue missions. It's all here. Carefully hidden. Compared to the Taylor Homes, it is tiny but inside it is crowded. They would have taken me back to Reed, but time has run out; the paperwork has been lost; fourteen days have passed. Rules of the game: If you can get away from anywhere and stay gone for over two weeks they staff you out and you were never there. They couldn't put us back in Reed so they carted Tanya off to a prison somewhere for killing her parents and they put me in a group home in the Taylors called Stevenson House. I learn to exist as best I can.

In the Robert Taylor Homes I get my first tattoo, a large dagger on my left shoulder blade. My roommate Cateyes gives it to me with a sterilized pin and a small bottle of india ink. We are badly drunk while he does it. The dagger is crooked. It is different from the gang symbols that mark everyone else's arms. Stevenson House is covered with blue-ink tattoos. I get beat up, I have the shoes stolen off my feet at gunpoint at the Garfield train station and I walk home in the snow wearing a pair of socks. In Stevenson House we stay up all night shooting dice, emulating the men down on their knees in front of the liquor store. The staff leaves us to our own devices; we occupy the upstairs, they occupy the downstairs. We play dice for T-shirts, notebooks, handmade pipes, bullets, sunglasses, Adidas, picks and combs, whatever we have. We make like the rest of the neighborhood, holding the dice in our palm, blowing on them for luck saying things like, "C'mon mamma. Be with me now." When someone loses all their clothes and knives and whatever else they have they throw a fit, kicking the wall, screaming at the ceiling. But it is all an act. We never fight over a game of dice. The projects are loaded with violence, but not when men are throwing dice.

I don't bother going to school. Nobody does. School is a myth, a fine place to get shot. I hang out with Craig and John and Craig protects me from becoming a teardrop under somebody's eye. Craig's mother comes for him every Sunday dressed in nice clothes and takes Craig off to church. I write poems that John performs as rap songs to everyone else. I write funny rhymes for John, "I forgot about cookies, I had a bunch, and that was just for sixth-period lunch," and everybody laughs and claps. Then Craig is taken off in a car with flashing blue lights and John is too fat to protect me and I prepare myself to be sliced up.

I meet once a week with my counselor, Willie. To get there I walk along State Street almost to the trains at Sixty-Third. His office is on the ground floor of one of the Taylor buildings. He always welcomes me with a big smile and we sit down to play a game of chess. His chessboard is expensive looking with marble pieces. Sometimes, while we play, there is a knock at the door and Willie hands someone a package or takes a package and casually throws it on his desk. After they take Craig away I tell him that I'm going to get cut, then I trade a pawn across the center of the board. He puts his fingers together. "Let me see what I can do, Paul. I'd hate to have no one to play chess with. Maybe we can keep you alive for a few more months." He takes my pawn from the queenside with his bishop. I am in trouble now.

In the Robert Taylor Homes if you kill someone you tattoo a teardrop under your eye. The guys that hang out in front of Willie's office have chains of them running down their faces onto their necks, noble savages, hungry, feared. Others stand on the street corners, arms folded, tattooed tears streaming down their faces. You make the decision in the Taylors. Once you kill someone you can never go back. I make the decision, I take my beatings. I never kill anyone.

Six months have passed since they took Tanya away and stuck me in the Robert Taylor Homes.

Yesterday I found out I would be leaving the Robert Taylor Homes. I was not the only one. I watch from a corner of the room in the dark. I see Cateyes get out of his bed, tuck a knife in his pocket. He walks over by my bed, his muscles taut, his chest slashed by moonlight. I can smell him. I see my bed from the dark corner of the room. I see the sweat come to his half-naked body. I study the silhouette of his knife, the moonlight reveals scars, hard puffy marks along his ribs. Then he walks out of the room. Water runs in the bathroom down the hall. He comes back in, puts his knife in a drawer, and goes to sleep. I stand in the corner all night long.

The Robert Taylor homes constitute an entire country. Today I am leaving that country, transferred up north as if by some act of God, to a nicer home, a specialized group home in a nice neighborhood with a front lawn. I don't know who ordered it or why. Some benevolent social worker in a DCFS office maybe slipped the pencil, misread a form. My file was transferred, I was moved, my yellow envelope switched from one drawer to another. Today it is over. From now on, it will be quiet.

4. Broken

The air rushes in the window and fills my lungs. Music plays from the car's radio. My caseworker's got her hair up in a bun and the streets roll by like movie credits.

"This is a specialized group home, Paul." I nod my head. A specialized group home means there is a foster parent with a foster license who watches the home and supervises a staff. She is paid by an agency. Specialized group homes are for kids that cannot be placed in a foster home but are more manageable than kids placed in group homes. A specialized group home like this will take a mixture of private and public kids but only kids that are low risk. Somewhere along the way I became a good bet. "Pretty lucky for you," she says. "I wouldn't get kicked out of this one."

I open my mouth and stick my head out the window. Nobody gets a second chance. I pull my head back in. My hair tickles the roof of the car. She turns away from the road for a second fixing me with dead blue eyes. I stare back at her. "Were you good-looking once?" I ask.

"Look. Don't get thrown out of this home. No one else is going to take you. This is a nice home, the end of the line, and I don't have the time for you. I have fifty-six children in my caseload. All day long the phone is ringing and it's the police or the firemen. Yesterday a boy on my list threw a twelve-year-old girl off the roof of a building in Cabrini Green. If you get thrown out of this one you will be without a home and without a worker and they'll just lock you up in Juvi until you're 18." I wait for the punchline.

"Yeah, well," I tell her. "Not your problem, right?"

"Not anymore," she answers.

We leave the south side, past the Field Museum and the Shedd Aquarium. Along Lake Shore Drive we pass the Ebony Jet Building, the Drake Hotel, the Sears Tower, the Standard Oil Building and the John Hancock Building. Then there's Wrigley Field, a string of twenty-five-story condominium buildings as Lake Shore Drive ends. She drives me past two-flats and three-flats where the grass is noticeably greener into a neighborhood that is almost entirely composed of short houses, up tight against one another, like people waiting in line, separated by three-foot fences.

She pulls into a driveway on a quiet street. The block is full of houses with front lawns and one three-story apartment building. We step out of the car. I watch her legs and then follow her under an archway, beneath cracked white paint, a cigarette butt in the corner of an otherwise spotless porch. A fat woman stands behind the door and first takes my caseworker's hand and then mine. The two retire to some room while I stand with my bag. There are four windows in the living room, a couch and a television. I toss my bag on the couch. Nobody else is here. It's a school day. All of the other kids must be in school. I run my hand along the top of the television set and wonder how much I could sell it for.

Anthony and I sit on the roof of my new house passing a pipe back and forth. Anthony is my new roommate. He wears a denim jacket with bright silver buttons and an Iron Maiden patch on the back. He's chubby with a fat suburban face. Long honey hair spills over his shoulders and halfway down his chest. This is the only group home he has ever lived in. He is private, meaning his parents put him here. I am public, meaning I did something bad, meaning I don't have parents. Legally the State of Illinois is my parents. Nicer homes like this sometimes have kids like Anthony, sometimes kids like me. He passes the pipe. Anthony has clean fingers. In the room he has a radio by his bed, a guitar, and a collection of rock and roll tapes.

"If you need any I can get it for you," he lets me know. I pull on the pipe. Anthony runs a brush through his long blond hair. "You can call me Ant," he tells me. "That's what everybody calls me. That's my name."

"What are you doing here, Ant?"

He shrugs his soft shoulders. If he had been on the south side they'd have eaten him alive. No, they ate me alive. They would have killed him. I lasted six months. He would have lasted a day.

"Seriously. What are you doing here? Your parents don't like you?"

"They don't want anything to do with me. I was living with my grandma. I got arrested with a bag of marijuana so they put me in here."

"Like a punishment?"

"Guess so." He passes the pipe to me again and I take another hit. "You have to watch out for Tracy," Ant tells me. "She's a bitch."

"She looks like a bitch," I tell him.

"She is a bitch." He takes a hit. A warm breeze passes off the street. It's the smell of marijuana and Chicago. "She'll go through your stuff when you're not around. If you piss her off she'll lie to your case-worker. Everybody thinks she's a dyke."

"You hate her, huh?"

"She's so fat two people could fuck her at the same time and never meet each other."

I chuckle and take another hit. It's good to know my roommate's a joker. The day is winding down. Across the street a man stumbles in the door of the only apartment building. The door clicks closed. Ant and I sit on our elbows.

• • •

Mather High School sits at the intersection of Peterson and California behind a large expanse of green lawn. There are two base-ball diamonds and a beat down playground as well as two tennis

courts without nets. There is a basketball court. The high school is
blue-gray concrete, one story, like a military compound or something.
Cement columns hold up the flat roof and the overhang that covers a
long strip of pavement running along the front of the building.
Hundreds of kids stand out front and funnel in and out of its doors.
In front of the school a closed street runs around a circular patch of
grass. Across the street from Mather High School there is a red brick
building that nobody knows is also a school. A few cars dot the
parking lot. No one would ever think there were children inside. No
one would ever think this small red brick building hidden by a tree,
across the street from the enormous Mather High School, was its own
separate, special school. The building is too small. The windows are
covered with curtains and you need to ring the buzzer to get inside.
But here it is, another holding pen, another layer of disguise. Staring
into the school, this short red building, I build barbed wire and bars
around it and decide that is what it looks like where Tanya is.

I meet caseworkers, psychologists, and the school principal. I go
through a battery of tests. Nervous songs dance in my head. Every
worker asks the same questions. They know the answers, the files sit
in their laps. They want to know about the abuse, the neglect, it gets
them hot. I hold out and they wriggle in their chairs. I think my story
isn't tragic enough for them, not juicy enough for the novel they are
writing in their mind. How many times in a day do they hear 'handcuffs' and 'radiator' in the same sentence? The one question they
always ask is, "What about your father? Tell us about your father."
They ask about my father with malicious jealousy. They just can't wait.

"Did he drink?"

"No."

"Did he do drugs?"

"No."

"Did he hit you?"

"Don't you already have this written in your file?"

I do not want to talk about my father. It is a boring subject. I want
to talk about Tanya. I tell them I forgive my father, I don't care about
my father. They ask me if I would be willing to go back with him. I
say, "No." They cloud me with their questions, prodding and prying,

taking notes. It is their job to be interested. I play my role and keep my information tight. I give them all the same story. I answer only the questions asked. I never tell them how it makes me feel.

One little old lady asks me if I am lying. She sits in her chair; her little legs dangling off the edge; her pointy black shoes angled towards the floor. She is the smallest woman I have ever seen.

"Why would I tell you if I was lying? That doesn't make any sense."

She frowns at me. "Paul, you're not on trial. We want to help you as best as we can but we cannot help you without your cooperation."

"Does that mean I don't have a right to an attorney?"

She doesn't like my answers; nobody does. I dig in. I grasp the seat, I squeeze the chair with my fingers. I want my fingernails to pop off. And then I throw up.

The school nurse comes. The maintenance man slops up the puke. The nurse takes my temperature. A Spanish girl walks by the door once. I am white. The blood is gone from my face. "Have you been feeling ill?" the nurse asks me.

"Don't you know that moving is the most stressful thing?" I tell her.

I've met the principal, the social workers, the teachers. I've done another inkblot test; it still looks like chicken.

I sit the rest of the day in a chair with a magazine full of short stories. They bring me water. The nurse wears white shoes. She is young and pretty, maybe only five years older than me. But I look older. I'm fifteen but people tell me I look almost thirty. I'm weathered. Nurses always look like they want to take you home but they never do.

The wind blows Ant's long hair back; keeps his denim jacket open. His chubby fingers play with the silver buttons on the dark blue coat. He's standing in front of the school with the Spanish girl. "This is my girlfriend, Maria."

Maria wears all pink; pink shorts, a pink shirt, pink earrings, pink lipstick. She looks like an unopened piece of candy. Her dark hair is done up like a little girl's.

"Hi Paul."

"Hi yourself."

"So you'll be starting school with us on Monday." She is trying to be friendly. A pretty girl with a pretty smile. She has some hard lessons coming. Group homes are hard. She's going to learn what other people want and what she needs.

"Yeah, it's not impossible."

Maria smiles at me. "See you then." She walks away from us and I look at Ant.

"Heard you threw up in the psych's office today."

"She deserved it," I tell him. We walk down California Avenue. We stop in front of a store and Ant combs his hair back looking at his own reflection. I look at my reflection and run my hand over my head.

"Why'd you throw up?"

"I don't know." The bus passes us by filled with kids from the normal high school across the street. They stand and sit in the big green bus. They wear bright red bandannas and the bus advertises some soon-to-be-released film. "I throw up all the time. Food doesn't sit well with me."

"What do you think of Maria?" he asks.

"She's your girlfriend."

"She's cute though, huh."

"You fuck her?"

At Thorndale he points to a light-gray three-story apartment building and says, "That's where she lives."

"That?"

"Yeah. That's the girl's home. They have twenty girls in there."

"Looks like an apartment building."

"Who would know," he agrees.

The weather is nice again. It's early spring. We walk past a grammar school on Clinton, then past The Pita House. "Hi guys." It's Jonathan, the semi-retarded kid from our home. There are only five of us in the home, Ant, Jonathan, Eric and Phillip who are both in grade school, and myself. In the last home I was in, Stevenson House, there were thirty of us. Sometimes we called Stevenson House the Warehouse because there were so many of us.

Jonathan is very dumb. He's the same age as me and Ant. "We made cardboard houses in art class today," he tells us.

"That's nice," Ant let's him know. "Have you considered moving into one of them?"

The three of us walk on for a bit until something catches Jonathan's attention and he goes skipping off.

My teacher has a long mustache that droops down his face. Gray stubble dots his cheeks. He wears a tweed jacket; his hair is curly and messy, like mine, but gray. Perhaps I will teach classes one day to behaviorally disturbed children. When he talks, he talks to the girls. He stares right at them just below the chins. He wears a wrinkled shirt and a loose tie. I think he is one sick bastard. I sit here with six other kids. This is the smart class again. Maria and Ant sit in the not-so-smart class down the hall. Past that, Jonathan sits in the other end of the building with the kids wearing bicycle helmets, drooling on their shirts, building Lego houses. Downstairs is the grammar school, Phil and Eric are down there with ten other kids.

We do some work in a workbook. Basic stuff. Easy. Basic division, single-digit multiplication. We break for lunch at twelve.

Ant, Maria, and I share a table. The lunchroom is in the basement and has red brick exposed walls. It looks like the outside of the building. We eat sandwiches that Tracy made for us, and we smoke. Someone's art project is taped to the wall, a poster board with a picture of a smiley-faced girl with curly hair. Maria brought her own sandwich from the girl's home, peanut butter and jelly, a bag of potato chips. There are about twenty kids in the room with us and smoke from all the cigarettes hangs along the ceiling. Everyone's got a story.

"You know…" I say to be casual, to show off. "When a new guy steps into a room like this, it's like there's a new cowboy in town." Maria covers her mouth. Ant chews his food. "Take those guys over there." I nod towards a table. Four guys eat their lunch, smoke cigarettes. A few girls hang around.

"That's Breen and Larry," Ant says. "Don't mess with them."

I put my sandwich down. I don't think there's enough excitement in my life. "You a virgin?" I ask Maria.

"What?"

"I wouldn't go out with a girl if I wasn't having sex."

Ant turns scarlet red.

"Maybe that's why you don't have a girlfriend," Maria tells me.

"What makes you think I don't have a girlfriend?" I ask her. I cock my head. She gives me a tiny smile. Ant stares at the table.

"One time I ran away from a locked facility with a girl."

"How far'd you get?"

"You want to know how far we got. We lived in a fucking toolshed and conned nuns out of blankets and baloney sandwiches. We made it as far as cardboard boxes. How fucking far have you ever gotten?"

This is not where the action is. I push away from the table. "I'm going for a walk. This place sucks." I kick my chair and it falls and skids across the linoleum floor. Everyone looks up for a moment and then goes back to their bananas and potato chips and peanut butter and jelly sandwiches. "Yeah, look at the new guy. Look at the new guy kicking a chair just like the rest of you psychos on a permanent restraining order. Hey, anybody got any Thorazine I can borrow?" Nobody pays me any attention and I run up the stairs and out of the building.

Outside a breeze cuts across Mather Park. Across the street the Mather High School Football Team practices in full pads, running into padded statues. I light up. I wonder if they know about us. I wonder if when they walk by they wonder about that red brick building across the street. I imagine them looking at the screened-in windows, the doorbell with no name on it. I imagine them counting the bricks, standing at our school, pushing their fingers along the wall. I don't think they do.

The group homes don't exist. And below the group homes, there are these places they put you when even the group homes won't take you. These places are so far gone, it's difficult to remember once you're out. Children's shelters, beds stretched thirty to a room, powdered eggs, no one in charge, no one knows what's going on or when you will get out or who you should ask until one day a car comes along and picks you up and you just try to forget. Adolescent mental health facilities, juvenile correctional centers, sub-programs of sub-programs funded by unknown neighborhood institutions occupying rooms on top of ghetto tenements with a desk and a pool table and a blanket in the corner. These places are so far gone, so invisible against the blues and yellows of the city street, it's difficult to remember, impossible to trace your way back, to find the opening in the circle. I can see the real world from where I stand. I can see the real world in football pads running into padded statues across the street. I can see their game. I can see the real world from here. The real world is just on the other side of the street.

Smoke curls into my bangs. I've been wearing the same pair of jeans for months. I'm so sick of everything. I throw my cigarette into the gutter. Lunch is over. It's time for gym class.

The teacher puts his hand on my shoulder. "Are you feeling better? It's difficult coming into a new place and it's normal to take some time to adjust."

"So I'm just like everybody else, huh?"

I don't know why all the teachers in this school have mustaches. We play basketball. There are ten boys in the class so it's an easy five-on-five. I'm just another stiff white kid here. A couple of kids seem to move the ball alright. Ricky, with worse acne than me, Terrance, who is thin and tall. We run up and down the court. Boneheaded Tony talks a bunch of trash and never scores.

After class we change back into our normal clothes, sweaty and sticky underneath our T-shirts and jeans. We change behind a series of partitions. There are no showers, no lockers. Larry says, "You can play a little. You'll be on my team from now on." I look at Larry. He was sitting at that table in the lunchroom. I size him up and down. He's a big boy, big arms. We step out into the hallway.

"I'm not your puppy dog," I tell him.

He puts his hands to his sides. There is going to be a fight. A lady with large blonde hair comes walking through the hallway. "You must be Paul. I've been looking for you. I'm your counselor." She extends her hand, which I take but keep my eyes on Larry. "If you have a minute let's talk."

• • •

I got a pulse. I got a problem.

I step into gym class. I hit Larry immediately. The gym smells of antiseptic. Larry hits me back and I see stars. It's a good punch. I feel the next one before I see it and I go down on the wood. I hear a whistle, then a footstep.

Larry's pinned down by Mr. K and some other teacher; he's screaming something. I stand up and my eye feels like a plum. Larry struggles; his lip is split and I feel my knuckles.

"What's wrong with him?" I ask Johny, the tall Mexican kid next to me.

"You punched him in the mouth."

"Would it help if I apologized?"

"I don't think so."

I pull on the bottom of my shirt. Larry says something. He convinces somebody. He walks out of the room flanked by two teachers. They keep their hands close to his arms.

The lunchroom reeks of bacon and cigarettes. Maria touches my eye with her pinky finger. Ant takes a bite out of a bacon sandwich Tracy made for him and a big glob of mayonnaise falls on his pants.

"I told you not to mess with Breen and Larry."

"I didn't want it hanging over my head."

"Who started it?" Maria asks.

"He said I was a good basketball player. He said he wanted me on his team."

Larry enters the room and a silence falls on us like a blanket.

People want to know what's going to happen. I want to point them across the street. There's another high school with one hundred times as many students and they don't even know we exist. Across the street they have organized dances, sports teams. They have gangs and guns and crack cocaine. It's a loser school with metal detectors at the door. But someone from that school is going to turn out OK, and nobody here is going to turn a nickel into a dime. So what if I punch Larry in the mouth or Larry punches me? How could it possibly matter? But I don't say anything except to focus on Ant and let him know, "Ant, you moron, you've got a tablespoon of mayonnaise on your pants."

Larry sits with Breen at their table. Maria says, "Go make things OK."

I laugh. "Troubled?" I ask her.

We go back to our silences. When I finally stand up it's been too long and nobody notices anymore, until I start to walk away from the door and towards the back of the room. I stand over Larry who doesn't even look up. I say, "I'm sorry...about that."

"Fuck you," he lets me know.

"Fuck you too," I let him know back. And I'm going to walk outside and test the grass but as I'm walking away a chair takes my legs out from underneath me and I fall backwards to the floor and my head cracks on the linoleum.

It's not over. After school, in the alley, ten or twelve kids watching, smoking cigarettes. Larry and I go at it. It's a cool day. The sky is patterned with soft white clouds and summer is looming on Chicago with its sticky, cotton T-shirts gluing to your frame heat. The first shot Larry lands my mouth breaks over my teeth, I swallow the blood, the world goes quiet.

Larry is big and strong. Larry knows some things. Then he misses, and I kick his knee and a sound comes, a POP, loud, then silence again. I hit him flush.

I leave Larry on the ground. I don't kick him. His leg is bent awkward and one of his friends has run off to call an ambulance. I walk away with Ant next to me and I light up a cigarette.

At home Tracy says, "You're not going outside for a week, except to go to school!" She's spitting as she talks and I wipe it off my cheek.

"That's fine by me," I let her know. "Nothing out there but a bunch of sickos."

Right then she hauls off and smacks me. I hear a plate break in the kitchen and my cheek burns. "You know," I say. Tracy turns on her heels and walks away, a bulldog, short and thick. I watch her legs, like tree trunks, her fat feet spring down the carpet. I stand in the doorframe, ready to go upstairs, into my bedroom. I continue, "I'm just getting tired of all this violence. I'm tired of it. I'm not a violent person and I don't think people should communicate this way."

That's what I tell Larry in the morning. "I'm tired of my lifestyle."

"Fuck you," he says. He's standing on crutches, we're in front of the school. The green bus pulls past us, down the street it unloads its precious cargo.

"Is that your standard response to everything?"

His buddy Breen comes walking up. Breen and Larry live in the Spaulding House on the other side of Bryn Mawr and hang out with the Spaulding and Bryn Mawr Royals.

"You better get the fuck out of here," Breen says.

"I'm gonna whoop your ass when I get off these crutches."

"No you're not. I'm not fighting anymore 'cause I'm tired of it."

"Get out of here," Breen pushes my chest and I stumble back towards the bushes. I steady myself.

"You know, when they first grabbed me, man, I had been homeless for like a year, and I was depressed. I was so fucking sad. Then they put me in a mental hospital." Breen and Larry look at me. "Seriously. A mental hospital. Can you believe it? And there was this guy, French Fry, who tried to burn himself to death and I had this therapist who was always flirting with me, showing me her legs, trying to fuck with my head. But then I totally fell for this girl. I ran away with this girl and they took her away from me. Put her in some jail or something. I miss her a lot, man. I think about her all the time. Always. They put me in the Robert Taylor Homes. The fucking Robert Taylor Homes. You know what I mean? Do you know how fucked up that was. Then I wasn't depressed anymore, I was angry. I was angry because they took my girl. You'd be angry too. I'm not fighting anymore. If I have to fight I'll just shoot you."

"You got a gun?" Larry asks.

The days pass at Campbell house. In school we do crafts and we play basketball and volleyball. Once a day someone has to be restrained and the rest of us play tic-tac-toe or smoke cigarettes. At night I hang out with Ant and sometimes Maria. We smoke pot on the roof of the home. Occasionally we get our hands on a bottle of something. We watch a lot of television. Coming home we're expected to enter through the back door. We're also required to have dinner together at six p.m.

The dinner table. Sunday night. Tracy has gone home. In her place is Starla. Starla has big eyes, large breasts. She has just graduated from college and will be watching the house on the weekends. Phillip and Eric are playing in the yard. I put up a basketball net for them yesterday. It had been sitting in the basement.

"Well Paul, this is our first dinner together." Her food still sits on her plate. She hasn't touched it. A piece of fried chicken. A small bowl of split pea soup she made from a big can. Starla looks like a substitute teacher, a sucker, a peach.

"Where's your father?" I ask her.

"He's back in Normal."

"What?"

"Normal, Illinois."

"What does he do?"

"He's an electrician." I wait for her to say something more. She doesn't.

"None of you have been in a real group home," I say. "This is not real. This is bullshit. You should check out where I've been. You guys don't have a fucking clue." Starla smiles awkwardly. Ant goes out to the back porch.

"You don't have to be tough with me, Paul. I know you're tough." Starla has a kind face, kind cheeks.

I wait for a second to see if Starla asks me about my father. When she doesn't I say, "Don't you want to know about my father? Or do you already know? Did you read it in my file?"

"Yes. I read it in your file."

"I'd like to read your file."

"I don't have a file," she says.

"Well, that doesn't seem fair. *Everybody* I meet has already seen my file, they know me, but I don't know anything about them."

Ant comes back to the table. "Want to have a smoke?" he asks me.

It's a sunny day. Phillip and Eric are beating the shit out of each other in the grass. Eric pins Phillip and hammers him three times in the mouth. Eric stands, takes the basketball, throws it towards the net.

Phillip cries in the grass, bleeding from the mouth. Phillip is private, like Ant. One day he will go back home. This will all be a quiet and closed chapter for him. Eric is public, like me. One day he will get kicked out of here and he'll go down into the hole.

Ant and I play checkers in the smoking room. I try to get him to play chess but he doesn't want to learn how. We're playing with flying kings and I'm not paying attention so he beats me.

"Ha," he laughs.

"Pretty funny."

"Play again?"

"Alright."

Tracy walks into the room waving away the smoke. If it was up to her we wouldn't smoke at all; but the agency says we have to have a smoking room, even at school. So that's one thing that's good about our school too. She frowns at us and Ant looks away. He never looks Tracy in the face.

"You have a phone call, Paul."

"I do?"

"And it's after eight. No phone calls are allowed after eight."

"My bad. Guy or girl?"

Tracy walks away without answering.

"I guess she's not your secretary," Ant chuckles.

I grab the phone in the living room and Tracy relaxes into the couch. "They said you got tossed, kicked. Said you got picked up by some new house down on the North Side." I hear a match strike on the other end of the line.

"Justin!"

"Hey man. So you like your new home?"

"Yeah. It's a nice place."

"You remember that trucker outside of Los Angeles?"

"Sure, I remember."

"Fucking bastard, that one. Things like that will keep us together forever. Shared experiences." I hear him inhale. "I got put in a place called Edison Park. It's just outside of the city."

"How is it?"

"It's OK. I've got a full day pass coming. Let's hook up, you cock."
I hang up the phone.

Ant and I smoke a joint on the roof. "I have this friend," I tell him.
"I hope so," he says coughing up smoke.
"I've known him since kindergarten. We both ran away from home at like the same time and we hung out a lot on the street even though a lot of times he would stay with girls he would meet. He's kind of fucked up. Total drug head. Thanks." I take the joint from Ant and have a pull. "The cops were looking for him for breaking into a basement and so we hitchhiked to Los Angeles." I hand him his joint back. "But that didn't really work out too well, though I got to see a lot of the country."
"You hitchhiked to Los Angeles? Wow."
"Yeah. It was pretty crazy."
"So he's a drug addict and a thief?" He inhales the last of the joint and flicks the roach into the gutter.
"Well, he always denied breaking into the basement. You know how cops are. All the chinks look the same to them. But Justin's one of those guys can keep a secret to the grave."
"I hate people like that," Ant says.
"Shut up," I tell him. "So I haven't heard from Justin in years because we got arrested in Las Vegas and of course they saw he had a warrant out for him. Now he's in Edison Park."
"I've heard of Edison Park. It's rough."
"Yeah. And he's just a skinny Chinese kid. But he likes to fight."
"So he's a thief, a drug addict and a fighter. Nice Friend."
"What do you know? You're from the suburbs. Things are different in the city."
"I gather." He hands me a cigarette and we both light up.
"Think we're going to get lung cancer?" I ask.
"At this rate," he replies.

Lying in bed I replay Justin's voice. Ant sleeps across from me. I remember a road that stretched on forever and never stopped. I remember the cops looking for Justin and I remember standing on

Pratt and California and deciding it was time to leave. We had been homeless for almost a year at that time. We decided to hitchhike to Los Angeles where it was warmer. We were going to be beach bums.

That was over two years ago. We never made it to the beach and somehow, everything changed. Instead of the beach I landed in a mental hospital and Justin landed in some jail. By the time we were arrested in front of Caesar's Palace, Las Vegas, Nevada, it was too late.

I remember a guard came to get me at four o'clock in the morning. He brought me into a large room with silent police officers peddling away at various papers in a thin light. A dark blue table ran the length of the room. Spooky.

"We only have four dollars in the runaway fund," the fat cop told me. "That's not enough to get you back to Chicago. You better stay another week."

"I'll be OK," I told him. "I don't eat much."

They gave me four dollars and all the things I had in my pockets when they arrested me: matchbooks and bus transfers.

"Can I say goodbye to my friend?" I asked.

"OK."

I was taken down a long corridor. The cop rapped on a door and then opened it. Justin looked up from his bed, the other boy buried his head underneath the pillow. The room was dirty white with dirty white bars on the windows. We left our shoes outside the rooms and slept in the clothes they gave us, brown T-shirts, pants without pockets.

"I'm getting out," I told him.

"How come they're letting you out and not me?" he asked.

"I don't know." Then the guard hurried me back to the main office.

A man put handcuffs on me and drove me to the bus station. The neon cowboy waved to us from a cheap downtown casino. Dark gaming halls opened their doors to the street and flannelled suckers marched with crunched faces and beaten hands stuffed in their pockets. I thought to myself, "Las Vegas sucks."

"You can take the handcuffs off me," I told the man. "I'm harmless."

"You're lucky your hands aren't behind your back like they're supposed to be."

At the Trailways station he sat with me waiting for the bus to arrive. We sat silent, like we didn't like each other. The handcuffs were still on and I sat on the bench and people stared when they walked by. Already I missed the clean pants and shirts of the correctional facility. My old jeans were filthy, caked in mud from our long trek across the American wilderness.

When the bus pulled up he took the handcuffs off me. "Be good," he said.

"I will," I told him. He gave me a bus ticket and then left the station.

"I don't have to leave," I thought to myself. "I could stay here." I bought a pack of cigarettes at the machine with two of my four dollars. Then I got on the bus bound for Chicago.

• • •

Justin's train rolls into the underground station at Kimball. When the train leaves Justin and I stand ten feet away from each other. The Kimball station is round like a missile silo. The sound from the street filters into the underground.

I smile from the beautiful irony of the writing on the wall. Justin looks the same. He is still good looking and thin, the way he was lying in his cell that night. His long black hair falls past his shoulders and onto his leather jacket. But the writing's on the wall behind him, spray-painted in enormous black letters: 'THIEF', and Justin smiles back at me, not seeing what I'm seeing. I start to laugh, I can't help myself. Justin smiles awkwardly.

We embrace. We hold onto each other, his shoulders. I smell his hair. His long, thin arms hold onto me. California is a long way away. A couple of runaways, lost by the highway. A truckstop in East L.A. Trucks full of carpets. I remember the names, Bekins, Mayflower, United Trucking. The trucks painted in dim, dirty colors, dirty orange, dirty green, the truckstop itself like an oasis of filth and the streets stretching off of it, its tributaries. Behind Justin the writing is still on the wall. A warning to every group home brat, a precursor to doom and the inevitable. Justin would never understand.

"Hey baby," he says, ridiculing our closeness; our faces are almost touching. "What you wanna do?" We step up the stairs and out to the streets.

In the sun I get a better look at him. He is still thin, long black hair, black leather jacket. He looks at me too. Both of us smiling. It's hard to make new old friends.

We duck into the first 7-11 we see. I ask the guy behind the counter for a dirty magazine while Justin opens the soda pop cooler. The guy hands me a *Penthouse* and I open it to the spread. "She's pretty hot," I say. The guy behind the counter doesn't pay me much attention; I hear a freezer door close. "Let me see that *Hustler*." I feel the breeze of cellophane. The front door opens and closes and Justin is gone. The counter guy gives me the *Hustler*; I page through it; I catalogue the images in my memory. "I don't have any money," I tell him. I turn and I walk out the store.

A block up Justin hands me two packs of smokes.

"The south side was rough," I tell him, "but I didn't back out of any fights." Lies. I tell him of ghetto adventures, south side romances. All lies, I think he knows. Still, it's our act, and friends have to help each other. I tell him I was a white spot on a black sheet of paper. I tell him I was the only white kid for ten miles. I don't tell him about Tanya. I don't tell him about how stupid I was and how I thought for a moment we could live in a toolshed forever and be happy and then the next moment the world smashed us like a fist through a window.

"Some girl named Nora," he starts. But with him it's true. There's always a girl. He's just so good looking. It's his defining quality.

Finally, down on Devon we've walked miles and we're all caught up, as much said as unsaid. It's been years. We're content to sit in the park. He pulls a bottle of Night Train from his bag, and we get drunk.

"Do you remember," I start. I always start. Justin looks up from his collar, pupils moving to the top of his eyes. "When we were in kindergarten and you would come over and we would make up those Stories."

"I didn't do much. You made up the story and I would just go along with you." A soft wind rummages through our hair, like a current. The park, our park, Chippewa Park, stretches in front of us, and we are alone.

"We had decided we would run away. We would build an electric go-cart."

Justin shrugs it off. He looks annoyed. He wants to change the subject. We pass the bottle back and forth. It's full of strong, thick red wine. "Your father."

"Yours," I say back. "Forget it. The world is full of crazy fathers." The wine tastes good. I don't want to talk about our fathers.

Justin's father chased me down in his taxi, drove up on the lawns, tried to run me over, cornered me next to an old brownstone, hit me in the chest with a large stick.

"I never want to have a kid," I tell Justin. He looks up at me. "Fathers are just bad."

I'm so drunk I lay my head down in Justin's lap. He leans back and we sleep for hours in the park.

When we wake up I bring Justin over to the girls' home. Ant and Maria are there sitting on the stoop. We all say hello. I light up a cigarette. I hand one to Ant.

"Aren't you going to have one?" Justin asks Maria.

"I don't smoke," she says.

"What kind of group home do you live in?" Justin asks. We're joined by Susan, Maria's roommate. Susan's blonde and full of ignorance. She tries to look like Madonna by tying up her hair and wearing cheap fashion jewelry.

"I'll take a cigarette." I give her one. I go to light it for her. "No. I want him to light it for me." Justin lights her smoke but keeps his eyes on Maria. A car speeds down Glenview, men hanging out of their windows, the horn blasting.

"What you guys do?" Ant asks.

"Had a drink."

"Got any left?"

"'Fraid not."

"I know your sister," Justin says.

"Whose sister?" Susan asks. I want to tell Susan to shut up.

"How do you know my sister?" Maria says.

"She lives in Edison Park. Her name's Nora."

Small worlds, all of them.

Back at the train station Justin says, "That girl knows a thing or two." Justin pushes his hands into his sides. I think I should not have answered the phone when he called.

I feel the tops of my cheeks sag. "No. She's innocent. She doesn't know anything."

Justin laughs. "She knows some things." The train takes Justin away. The day fades into an uneventful week. And that fades into the next uneventful week. Just like nothing.

• • •

"You had a visitor today," Tracy says at dinner.

"Was she hot?" I ask and Ant laughs.

"*He* was quite large and black. He left a package for you."

"Where is it?"

"Finish eating your dinner first."

After dinner I'm sitting on the couch waiting for everybody else to finish eating. When they do Tracy drops a yellow envelope on my lap. The envelope has already been torn open. "Did you open this?" I ask. She doesn't respond. She stands over me, her legs slightly spread on either side of my foot, watching. I stare up over her large belly and breasts and pull my feet under me on the couch then I walk across the couch, jump down and walk away from Tracy and up the stairs.

In my bed I take the letter out. I don't get much mail.

Paul,

I'm writing this from a prison in downstate Illinois. I am in the cafeteria and we are all sitting six to a table. Remember how bad the food was in Reed? It's like that here. Oh God Paul, I miss you so much. I just want to hold you. I tell myself you are doing OK. You are a survivor. Don't let anyone tell you that you won't make it. If anybody can make it you can.

Things are fine. We have uniforms so everyone looks the same, which makes it easier. Hope you are OK. I wish you had come with me like you said you would. I've been reading books. We go to classes here but

*if they try me as an adult there won't be any more classes. I don't know
what they do to pass the time in the adult prisons but people here say
it's pretty bad. If they try me as an adult I'll never get out. I have a
cousin who visits me sometimes. He's nice but I don't trust him. I
trusted you. I am still waiting to find out if I will be tried as an adult.
The prosecutor wants to lock me up forever. She hates me. She looks
like the nun. Remember the nun? Sometimes I go to church here. They
like it if you go to church so you're less likely to lose privileges. I can't
tell you where I am right now because if I did and you didn't come
here it would kill me. Wait for me. You have to wait for me.
Tanya*

At the bottom of the letter is a picture of a bride and a groom, just
like the ones she used to draw in Reed. The letter has no return
address. I wonder how she knew where to send it. I fold it up tightly
and put it in my pocket.

In gym we divide into teams and play basketball. We are compet-
itive. Everyone in the room talks at once. We scream at each other for
making or not making shots. Johny raises his hands above his head
and proclaims, "I am a star."

After gym Maria and I go out by the monkey bars behind the
school. We don't bring Ant, Maria doesn't want to. She hangs from the
bars and I sit on the old blue bench. Roast beef from the Arby's on
Peterson poisons the air.

"I'm a banana," Maria says. "Do you want to peel me?"

Spring is still here. I peer back towards our red brick building and
the clouds beyond it and I think of the striped mountains behind the
desert. Maria is innocent but in the two months I've been here I've
seen her change. The girls' home is rougher than the boys' home. Her
eyes aren't as clear now. Her lipstick no longer matches her earrings.

"I'm breaking up with Ant," she tells me. My nose twitches.

"You've been talking with Justin?"

"Yes."

I'd like to peel her, like a banana. I'd like to pull her clothes off of
her. I'd like to untie her pink gym shoes and lay them in the dirt next

to the broken water fountain. I'd like to roll her black leggings down and see her underwear. I want to put my hands up inside her shirt while I kiss her mouth.

"What happened to that girl you said you had? You didn't used to look at me that way."

"You didn't used to know when you were being looked at."

Maria smiles slyly at me. Losing innocence can be like a drug sometimes. A bad drug. A bad habit.

"That girl got taken away," I tell Maria. "And I never saw her again."

"Two Answers," she says. It's a game we play where we each reveal exactly one thing about our past. Generally it's supposed to be something shocking, something that led to our current group home internment, but it doesn't have to. Since she announced it I have to go first.

"I slept on a rooftop for a year," I tell her. "Justin was with me a lot of the time."

"My grandmother used to make me go door-to-door asking for money to support her heroin habit."

"That's some sick shit."

She drops down from the monkey bars. "For some reason it doesn't seem that bad to me."

"I feel that way about my stuff too. When I lived at home I had a bed and my own bedroom but I think the rooftop was more comfortable, even when it snowed."

We sit on the bench for a while holding hands. If I were to be honest I would tell her something, something about basements, mental hospitals, a friend called French Fry, but I don't. Anyway, she's been talking to Justin and Justin is my best friend.

The summers pick Chicago like a ripe fruit. The home wants me to go to summer school. I tell them to forget about it; they couldn't teach me anything there. I ask the neighbors if I can work on the truck.

This is the only job I can do. I'm too young to work legally. Tracy likes it because she's sick of looking at my ugly face. I leave the house early in the morning and come back late. Tracy's always asleep when I come in.

I knock on the door at six in the morning.

"C'mon in." I'm given a cup of coffee. Shaka is putting on his shoes. Shaka is an enormous slab of a man. The old man, Mr. Alston, pulls on his suspenders. Mike, the salesguy, still looks drunk from last night. This is our crew. Shaka and I do the construction, usually tuck-pointing but sometimes cleaning out gutters. The old man owns the business and drives the truck. Mike goes door-to-door selling jobs.

The door to Shaka's bedroom is open and his girlfriend, Brandy, snores heavily. She is a beast of a girl herself. Bigger than Shaka even. Brandy is the old man's daughter and when Shaka hitched up with her he got himself a free place to sleep and a job.

Shaka and I sit in the back of the truck with the dry buckets, the pale cement barrel, hawks and slicks, the pallet and the paintbrush, while the wind blows the dust off our jeans. I love the air in Chicago's morning when the truck cruises down Chicago's longest streets: Western, Halsted, Ashland. I am in love with Chicago's streets. "Hey Shaka," I scream over the wind. "Did you know that Western is the longest street in Chicago?"

"How do you know that?"

"Because it starts at Howard and continues all the way, unbroken, to 124th where the city ends. Did you know I can pinpoint the numbers for any two streets in Chicago?"

"That's nice," he tells me.

"For example. If I knew you were at Daman and Peterson I could tell you that you are 2000 west and 6000 north."

We stop at McDonald's for more coffee and sausage biscuits. The old man pays. He grumbles something but I don't know what he's saying because he has no teeth. We slop down breakfast in fifteen minutes and go to the yard to pick up bags of sand and cement mix and dye. Shaka holds open the bag and I shovel in the mix. When the bag is full it weighs fifty pounds. At the site we unload the supplies: wheelbarrow, tools, buckets, fifty-pound sacks of sand and cement. I mix it all up with a hoe while Shaka sets chicken ladders and the other guys canvas for more work.

By the end of the day my shoulders are always burnt and peeling. We take down the ladders; the truck is waiting. Clean out the barrel, hose down the buckets, the truck takes us back to Campbell Street.

I meet Maria over at Price, the girls' group home. Price is not a specialized group home. There are thirty girls and four staff members on duty at any time. It's a rough place as rough as any guys' group home. That's because it is really hard for a girl to end up there. Most girls end up in foster care but some girls are too unmanageable for that and other girls are just unlucky. When I walk in Susan throws a phone at me and just misses my head. She is restrained. Maria comes out and hugs me. Behind her someone is screaming, "You fucking bitch! You stole my earrings." Maria rolls her eyes. "Let's get out of here," she says.

We head down to the Quick Stop. I buy us a couple of candy bars and cans of soda pop. We sit on the corner under the walk/don't walk sign. A beggar stands kitty-corner throwing up on a newspaper box. I light up a cigarette. Maria takes one out of my pack and lights it herself.

"You look thinner," I tell her.

"I want to be thin," she says. "I want to be like a model." Her cheeks are lower, her eyes are darker. She wears cheap makeup and cheap lipstick.

"You still seeing Justin?"

"You talk to him. You know."

"No. I haven't talked to him. I've been working."

"Yeah." She lets out a thin cloud of smoke, almost coughs, then catches herself. "I saw him last week." She coughs again. It's a bad cough. She coughs in her room at night. She coughs until she's choking. She coughs into her pillow.

"Look," I tell her. "I'm going to tell you something for your own good." I flick my cigarette at a passing car. "Don't have sex with him."

"I've never had sex with anybody," she lets me know. "How about you. Have you ever had sex?"

"Not yet. But I used to sleep with a girl. That's different though, you know. That's OK. But if you sleep with Justin he'll stick it in you while you're sleeping and you'll wake up pregnant. He's crafty like that. He's very crafty." The sun is beating down. I don't like the sun as much as most people and I'm hot in a pair of thick blue jeans and white T-shirt. Maria wears a short skirt, shorter than I've ever seen her wear, a little halter-top. She is looking like the group home now. "Let's walk," I tell her.

We go past the Dominick's on Pratt, where Tanya and I once ate the food they threw away, across Kedzie. We cross into the canal, through the trail, down by the water. I climb on a tree; Maria sits on a rock. A rat scurries along the edge of the water.

"I gave him oral sex. Does that make me bad?"

"What do I know about good and bad?" I light up a cigarette. She looks like she wants one. She is too young to smoke, I decide, and put them back in my pocket.

"But don't you still want to peel me, like a banana?"

"No. You're Justin's girlfriend. Besides, I never wanted to peel you," I lie. I lie. I lie.

"So what are we going to do?" she asks.

"What do we do everyday. Somehow the time passes. Everyday ends."

"I'll be happy when school starts again."

We sit in silence, admire the silence of the murky water. I pull on my hair. It is getting long. In my pocket I have thirty dollars, a pack of cigarettes, and a letter from my father. "Want to see a letter?"

"Sure."

I open it and Maria and I read it together.

Dearest Son,

I only did what was necessary and for your own good. I never meant to hit you, I was only using the necessary force to make the arrest. I realize now it was a mistake to give you a haircut. Please come and visit your old man who loves you so much you can only imagine. Letting you go was a mistake. I should have looked for you. You'll realize when you are older how much I loved you and how I had to do the things I did. I took care of your mother when she was sick and you were out doing drugs with your friends. Your poor father had it hard.

Love Always

"My father is full of regrets. I forgive him. He asks me to visit. I don't want to visit."

"I think he's a sick jerk."

I fold the letter up and put it back in my pocket.

We sit in silence. In her mind perhaps visions of grandma. Visions of closets and shit-stained dresses. We are deeply flawed. We are broken. School starts in a month and a half. One more month and a half on the truck. A rat scurries along the edge of the canal kicking up tiny pools of dirty water.

"You know, it occurs to me," I begin. "If we don't get our act together, we're fucked."

Maria lets out a tiny laugh. "I bet you say that to all the girls."

"I think I'm going to try to transfer to the normal high school across the street."

"Don't do that," Maria says.

"I have to."

"You won't fit in."

"I don't fit in anywhere."

"You fit in at our school. People like you."

We let the silence drift in again, set against the slopping puddles of the Chicago canal.

It's Sunday and Starla and I sit in the smoking room. Her boyfriend is in the living room watching a baseball game. I have Ant's guitar in my lap. The smoking room is hot and poorly ventilated, the windows closed, the shades drawn. I strum a couple of chords.

"How is your summer?" Starla asks me. Her skin is tan and smooth. She smiles when she talks. Her long brown hair runs past her shoulders.

"I don't like your boyfriend," I tell her. I strum on the guitar some more and then place it in the corner. "He doesn't pay you enough attention."

She squints and then smiles. "You know, Paul, when people have been together for awhile it's OK that they do not continually communicate."

"You like baseball?" I ask her. She shrugs her shoulders. It's her job to watch the house on the weekends. "I don't like baseball either," I tell her. "I think it's boring."

Starla lights a new cigarette off the one she has been burning. Starla has long, thin legs. "How is your summer job going?"

"It's OK," I tell her. "We just put cement between the bricks in people's houses. Mr. Alston says a lot of the work we do doesn't need to be done. But we do it anyway, for the money."

"That's doesn't sound very honest."

Now I shrug my shoulders. In the other room we hear clapping. "I guess someone scored a home run."

Starla laughs. "Don't be so cynical, Paul. You'll grow up an unhappy person."

Today we lay a roof down on Peterson. The old man has to rent a tar heater. We pour the tar on the roof and spread it with thick mops and I get tar on my jeans and Shaka tells me that tar never comes off of jeans, which makes me happy because now I have a pair of work pants.

The sun is full today and the tar and the hot roof make it even hotter so I work with my shirt off. "When are you going to cut that mop?" Shaka asks me.

"I don't think I will," I tell him and pull on my hair. Shaka's girlfriend Brandy waits for us after work in a halter top, thick sweat dripping down her fat, white arms.

Brandy, Shaka and I take a drive into the ghetto. Brandy drives her father's Pontiac Le Mans. It's an old beater of a car, red with a silver stripe running the length of its side.

"Paul worked hard today," Shaka says. I don't know why he is saying this about me since we both work hard every day and also smoke pot and cigarettes on the job.

"Father says you're a good worker," Brandy says to me.

"He works good for fifteen years old," Shaka says. "Hey Paul, why don't you quit school and work on the truck year round."

"I bet it gets cold in the back of the truck in the winter."

We pull onto Sesame Street and Brandy cops a bag of tic. "Hey baby," Batman says to her. Batman is their drug dealer. Shaka's shoulders tense up in his T-shirt. Brandy grabs the bag and reaches into her pocket for twenty dollars to hand over and just as Batman goes to grab the bill, his fingers touching the air inside the car, Brandy steps on the gas and the car screams forward. Gunshots ring through Logan Square and the back windshield crumples into dust. The wind kicks up through the front windows, pours out the back creating this vacuum and pulling my hair straight. I wonder if I've been shot. I take a deep breath from the gust of wind, swallow the wind as hard as I can and decide, no, I have not been shot. Listening in the wind I hear the laughter coming from the front seat and I join it. I join with the sound and smell and laughter of the wind.

Back at the apartment Shaka and I open beers and Brandy cuts us lines. The beer is crisp and good. Brandy pops a pill instead. I wait for them then do my line last. Brandy places an Elvis record on the turntable.

Nothing comes from the tic. Brandy lays out another large line and takes it up. Shaka and I watch from the back of the room. Brandy turns to us, her hair sticking out of her head in black wires, her enormous body taking up as much space as the dresser and the mirror, a long line of blood running from her nose and over her lips. "This shit's bogus," she says. "They fucking burned us. The fucking spics burned us."

"Can't trust the spics," Shaka says. "Got to deal with white people."

"I think Spanish people are white," I say.

"No they are not," Brandy tells me. "They're spics and they're brown and they're dirty lying fucking bastards." Her large hand comes down on the record player and the music stops and the record cuts in two.

"OK," I say and nurse my beer in the corner. Soon it's time to leave and I sneak across the street and into the home. School starts tomorrow, the summer is over.

Tracy knocks loudly on the door. "Summer's over! Get up. Go to school!"

Ant and I sit up, stare at one another. "Fuck you," I say to him. He throws a sock at my head and I dodge to the side rolling out of bed and hitting the floor. I fire socks back at him. I bunker behind my bed and he bunkers behind his.

"We will bomb you into submission," I announce, launching everything I can get my hands on, clothes, books.

"Never," he replies. "We will never surrender."

"You must. You must surrender and the conditions of your surrender include a universal acknowledgment of your homosexuality." A dirty sock hits me in the nose. "Hey, you bastard." Then a towel falls over my head. I realize I have lost the higher ground. I give in to Ant and we start getting ready for school.

Ant and I walk down the street. We come to our red brick high school. I look longingly at Mather High School across the street. A large crowd of students is filing through its double doors. And we enter by ringing the bell and being buzzed in. People exist this way, exist in buildings, other people don't know they are there. They exist in relation to, and also without the knowledge of, one another. Ant goes to his class but I wait a minute and stand by the window that looks out on California Avenue. There's a tree, a couple of storefront businesses.

Kids going to Mather pass by. They cannot see in for the gray film. They still do not know what is inside. I wonder why I know who they are and they do not know who I am. As I turn around I make my mind up. Then I see Larry and Breen. Maria passes behind them. Her face is thinner. Larry crosses his large arms across his chest.

"You have a good summer?" I say to them.

"You still want to fight?" Larry asks.

"No. I don't want to fight you. You're stronger than I am. Let's forget about it." Breen's eyes glisten behind Larry. I feel surrounded by Larry's cheap cologne.

I don't know how or why, but they leave, and nothing happens. They dissolve into the hallways, the classrooms. This has to be my lucky day.

I step past the secretary's desk. "Principal in?" I ask.

"He's busy," she replies. Her white shirt accentuates her dark skin. "First day of school. How are you, Paul? Did you have a good summer?"

"I was in a car and the back window got shot out. But it was a pretty good summer. I worked on a construction truck and made some money."

"Good for you, Paul."

I hang out on the gray chairs by the office. Parents for the private kids go in and meet with the principal. Private kids are fucked up and some live at home but go to our school. Group home kids go to the fucked-up school no matter what.

After an hour the principal finally sees me.

"How are you, Paul?" He has a big face, a big smile, big, chubby hands which lie on top of his desk.

"I'm OK but I'm being held back."

"Why do you feel that way?"

"It's just that I feel like I'm caught in this cycle. It's like a circle or something. I don't really feel like this is a school, it's more like we're being hidden here, which is OK for everyone else, but not for me."

"You feel you're different?"

"Don't you?" I ask him. "If I wasn't different who would I be? I'm not trying to be president I just want to go to a normal school."

The principal smiles at me. His big face seems kind enough. "So what are you proposing, Paul?"

"I have a reasonable offer for you," I tell him. "I want to go to Mather. And then from Mather I want to go to a University. If I get an A in every class I would like to go to the normal school across the street."

"Sure."

"I'd like for you to sign a piece of paper, saying it's OK."

"I can do that," he says. He smiles largely and his large hands write out our contract on a sheet of paper. He's a reasonable man and I like him. He doesn't think I'll do it. We both sign the bottom of the page. He thinks I'm a sucker and I think he's a sucker. Out of his window the last kid straggles in late and the principal leans back in his large brown chair. He lays his large hands across his belly. The principal smiles at me in an easy way and I know I'm through here.

At lunch I tell Maria what I did while I eat her sandwich and then her potato chips. "You're leaving me," she says. Her voice sounds hollow.

"You've lost a lot of weight," I tell her. Ant sits at the table in the back with Breen and Larry.

"I want to be thinner." I light a cigarette and hand one to her and then give her mine to light her own.

"I need to get out," I tell her. I touch her fingers.

And then she says, "I love Justin." She looks to me for a reaction. I hold strong. "Will you come out and see him with me this weekend?"

"Yeah. Of course. Sure. Love to." We smoke some more. "A person can't get an education here."

"You're leaving me," she repeats.

"How can I be fucking leaving you? We're not dating. You're Justin's." I rub my hand over my face. Ugly, ugly. I want to pound the table, smash a window, kick a lamp, tear up something important. "I can't leave you. Only Justin can leave you."

"Two Answers."

"My father handcuffed me to a pipe in the basement and called me an animal." I ball up the empty baggies and throw them in the trash.

"My uncle molested me repeatedly."

"Don't you think," I tell her, "that there are people out there with two parents, normal families. Don't you think about that?"

"You want to know what I think?" I feel her foot touch mine under the table. "I think you think they are better than you and you are jealous of them and want to be like them but you can't be because you're just a group home kid, like me. You can't be normal."

"I'm not the jealous type."

"I am," she says.

At the weekend I meet Maria in front of the convenience store. She wears a red skirt and shiny black nylons. We get on the bus at Devon and California. It takes us to a train station at Lawrence.

"I used to live over here," Maria tells me. "That was my grand-mother's house over there." She points to a string of unpainted bungalows anchored by a liquor store and a hot dog shack. The train passes them easily.

The train is wide open but Maria and I sit next to each other. I run my fingers over her face and trace out her features. I've made some bad decisions. I run a finger over her lips and she smiles and I smile and our train hustles towards strange and lost suburbs where Justin lives in a compound hidden from society.

We get off at Jefferson Park and board the Foster bus. We get off the bus at Park Ridge and cut across a green lawn, duck behind old brick buildings and a shiny Catholic church.

The homes of Edison Park form a square with large patches of grass between them. It's easy to see the functional nature of the setup, the dining halls, the school, and the residences. A self-contained childhood.

"This place is functional."

"What's wrong with that?" Maria asks.

"You know…"

"What?"

"Forget it."

"No. Tell me."

"Forget it."

"Don't be an ass or I'll stop loving you." She squeezes my hand. The dormitory stands in front of us. Next to it a handful of kids our age play basketball.

"You have the adult population. In a place like this that's comprised of nuns and a handful of do-gooders. They are in charge of another population, the kids, us. We have to do what they say because, on average, they make better decisions than we do."

Maria looks eagerly towards the door. The fall wind sweeps across the compound. I continue for myself.

"Of course, that doesn't leave any room for situations where the adult is mistaken and we're right. It's the only way a place like this can function but it's impossible especially with a large number of adults each with their own opinions of what a kid's responsibilities are."

"You're smart," Maria says sarcastically.

"Next time don't ask," I tell her.

Justin stands in the doorway and I look all around him for a sign. On Broadway in East L.A. there was a greasy spoon. Justin and I sat inside there and ate a basket of french fries and waited for a trucker to come back and pick us up. We had left our last bag in his truck. Justin told me that food never tasted as good as that basket of fries.

Then Justin told me the truck driver would not be coming back with our bag. I asked him how he knew and he shrugged his shoulders and looked down at the table. Then he started crying and told me the truck driver had molested him.

"How could he molest you when I slept right behind you?" I had slept just behind the seats in the cabin.

"He did."

I broke the sugar glass on the floor. "Why didn't you scream?" I asked. I remember pulling out a cigarette. "This is our last fucking cigarette. All of our cigarettes were in that bag." Trucks kept grinding by the streets outside the restaurant. We had no money. "Why didn't you scream?" I asked him. "There were two of us, only one of him. I just don't understand why you didn't scream."

Justin stands in the doorway with his thin brown arms pushed out against the doorframe. He smiles when he sees me and Maria. Maria looks up and almost runs to him. With his long hair he looks like a Chinese Jesus.

Maria puts her arms around him and they kiss. I look into his eyes, he stares at me behind her. He pushes away from her, not wanting to get in trouble. "Paul."

"Justin."

We step inside. The floors are brown and black linoleum tiles. An office stands immediately inside the door and an old black lady with graying hair sits behind a desk sharpening her pencil. She doesn't look up. There is dust on the walls. In the middle of one hallway a group of three kids stand in a triangle facing one another. There are evenly spaced dark brown doors with maybe four feet between each. The hallways go on to where I can't see the end.

"Do you feel like playing pool?" Justin asks.

"I don't mind."

In the basement he racks up the table. Justin is less afraid now. I hold on to a stick and he grabs Maria. She doesn't resist him. I look away. I open the small window a crack and the breeze — that fall breeze — cuts slightly into the room. It's sad. I turn back. They are against the wall, her red skirt is raised. His hands are inside her shiny black nylons. The carpet is green, the pool table is green.

I light a cigarette and wonder if this is for me. Are they putting on a show? I blow the smoke out the window but the wind blows it back in my face and now I'm worried they will know I was smoking inside. I flick the cigarette out into the bushes and sit down on a yellow plastic chair while Justin kisses Maria and sticks his fingers inside her skirt. I watch them. I watch his hands. I watch her legs, they cross, they squeeze his hands. Then they uncross.

I rack the pool balls. For a little while I was an OK pool player. I hit the cue ball as hard as I can and two balls come close to the holes but none fall in. I shoot at the balls but I keep missing and finally I give up. I'm a quitter.

I walk back up the stairs, past the hallways, past the black lady sharpening her pencil. I step into the bathroom, wash my hands, run my wet hands over my face, study the tiles. Two boys walk into the bathroom behind me. They stare at me and I stare into the mirror back at them. They both go into the same stall and close the door. Probably sniffing glue. The walls breathe, they exhale; the pores in my face open. I walk backwards slowly out of the door. In front of the home I light a cigarette. There are boys playing basketball in a tiny court, six of them. They wear hooded pullovers and jeans and old sneakers. I sit down on the steps.

When Justin and Maria come out we go for a walk through Park Ridge. "While you guys were playing pool," I say. "There was a fight on the basketball court. It was George."

"How do you know George?" Justin asks.

"We were locked up together. He beat me up once."

"He's tough."

"He hit this other kid. They were playing basketball."

"He shouldn't have done that," Justin says. "Now they won't let him go outside for a month." Oak trees shadow the well-dressed houses. Clean shiny cars sit in the driveway.

"For a month?" Maria asks.

"That's insane." We walk through the peaceful suburb of Park Ridge. I feel like the clean houses are lined up against us but Justin and

Maria just hold hands. We walk past confectioneries, corner drug-stores. I guess the neighborhood is so quiet because they don't let the kids out of the home. George cannot go outside for a month. I know Justin must have been really good in order to be able to go outside now. And he must have been good for more than a week. He must have been good for six months now.

"Isn't your sister in Edison Park?" I ask Maria.

"She was. They locked her back up in the mental hospital."

When we are done walking we are back at Edison Park and already there is a line of boys waiting for their meals from the dining hall. The line stretches out of the building and halfway across the lawn to the first residence hall. Maria goes to use the bathroom and I am left with Justin.

"We've got a lot of history, Paul." He waits for me to say some-thing. "We're like family. You're the only family I got. I think we'll know each other forever."

The sky is filling with light gray clouds.

"There will be a point," he tells me, "when we will be out of these crazy homes."

"They have crazy homes for adults too," I tell him.

"Always the cynic," Justin laughs.

Maria comes back and it's time for us to go catch our bus and Justin takes his place at the back of the food line and Maria and I, we walk away.

Falls are brief and sometimes gentle in Chicago. Ant and I sit on the roof under the tree. Ant smokes grass out of a cheap, tin pipe. He gives it to me and I take a hit and then hand it back.

"You're the model student now," Ant tells me. He pulls on the pipe some more. The street is dark, the houses lit by orange phosphorescent lights. Across the way the light is on in the apartment building where Alston construction is housed. It feels like years that I've been sitting on this rooftop getting high with Ant. In reality it's been six months.

"You know, you can get an A in every class without even doing homework," I tell Ant. "Take twenty minutes during lunch and do your assignments, run around the bases during gym."

"I couldn't be like you," he says.

In art class I try to draw pictures of a man and a woman getting married. But I am not good at drawing pictures. I trace my marker along the spaces in the wall when the teacher is not looking. I draw swirls on the large poster board. Since I met with the principal I have done everything right. I have lived up to my end of the bargain. I am going to go to the normal school and they are going to know who I am.

I draw circles. What shall I be? I write the word plumber inside the circles. The circles cross over one another. The colors blend. I fill the page with smaller and smaller circles. I write the word truck driver. Truck driver sounds fine, hitchhikers would be safe with me. I could be a banker. I use different colors. I use shades of blue and green. It is not a good picture. It is not even a good design. Perhaps the great artists started this way. They drew things that were not very good and kept at it until all of a sudden it was good. Maybe I am just one stroke away from a work of art. I write the word painter then I scratch it out. Therapist. I laugh. I draw a big circle around the whole page. Then a large purple circle just inside of that. I laugh some more. The other kids look up at me. I ignore them. I keep laughing.

"What are you doing?" the art teacher asks.

"I'm making a mess of my life," I reply, and I continue laughing, but nobody else laughs. I keep laughing just the same. The art teacher moves away. I will have to change my act when they put me in that normal school across the street.

I am in the living room. The phone rings. "Nothing is right, nothing is OK," Maria tells me over the phone line. Someone in the background screams out, "You bitch!" It sounds like there is a riot happening over there. The television is on and Jonathan and Ant and Tracy sit on the couch.

"Take it easy."

"I can't. It's all wrong." I hear something smash.

"What's going on over there?"

"I need to leave. I can't take it!" She screams into the telephone, I hold it away from my ear. It's late at night. My street is quiet. "It's my grandmother," she tells me.

"Your grandmother?"

"She used to make me kneel on grains of rice when she was mad at me. She'd bring home these men and they'd sneer at me sitting on the floor. They'd shoot heroin in front of me and once she kicked me in the face." Her voice is rising.

"Maria, you have to relax."

"I can't relax. I can't. Her boyfriends raped me all the time and she let them. Then she'd get jealous and beat me up. I hate her! I keep washing myself. I can't get them out. Why aren't you saying anything?"

"I don't know what to say."

"Well, say something."

"What? What should I say?"

"The walls are closing on me."

"Maria, stop."

"Screw you. You said you wanted to peel me. I see how you look at me. You think I didn't notice? I feel it when I sit on your lap. You're like them!"

I feel for a cigarette in my pocket. They are there but I am not allowed to smoke them in the living room. Tracy looks at me sideways and snorts.

Maria says, "You want to fuck me, don't you?"

"Maria listen…"

"You do. I know you do."

"Sure I do."

"I knew it."

"I'm only human."

She sounds calm now. Then she cries for a bit. I hold the line. "I'm messed up, I'll never be OK."

"Broken."

"Broken." We hold the line some more but there is nothing left unsaid. As we hold the line I think to say we'll work things out. I'll come over everyday. You'll see, I'll help you make it. But I don't say these things. The TV is going and that distracts me. And also, none of that stuff sounds true. And I hope Maria is just having an episode because we all have episodes and it's hard to tell with all this noise when someone is screaming because they're lonely and fucked up and need attention or when someone is screaming because they just fell off a cliff. Sounds the same. She whispers goodbye to me in a tiny, far-away voice. She says goodbye, in a voice that says things are OK but knows they never will be. Things will never be OK. You can't undo the past. I can't get her uncles out of her, her grandmother's boyfriends out of her. To tell her to deal with it would be the same as not understanding at all. It is no wonder they put us in these homes. They are not trying to help us. They know they can't. They are going to hold us until we are morally responsible and then wish us luck. I put the phone on the hook and sit down on the couch next to Ant. There's a movie on the television. Men with guns.

Maria is not in the lunchroom. I sit at our table against the wall. Ant sits with Breen and Larry at the end. It is a small room. I could go and sit with them. I sit next to the wall, tap my fingers on the table.

I reach in my bag and pull out a sandwich wrapped in plastic. Barbecue sauce stains the ends of the white bread. It looks like something bloody. I pitch it in the trash.

There are other kids in the room. There are maybe twenty of us here. The lunchroom is in the basement. We are one level below the ground. Susan sits two tables away with Darnesie, eating potato chips and looking around, nervous. Mike is in the corner with Ronny. Mike is talking to himself and Ronny ignores him.

I don't belong with these misfits. Joileene is brushing her hair. Before they put her in the home she was a high-priced hooker turning tricks for five hundred dollars a pull, living in a fancy studio down on the gold coast. Those old guys love the little girls. Then she got pregnant. I look at her and she waves and I wave back and she returns to brushing her hair.

I am a normal enough kid. I like sports. I have terrible skin. My mind wanders. I think about sex all the time.

A few drops of rain splash on the windows. Then a few drops more. I open my notebook on the table and write a few sentences. Maybe I'll write a letter to my social worker back in the projects. He came to the house to see me. He asked what had happened to me. I was being killed. I was standing in corners, trying to hold my breath. I was locking the bathroom door and trying to sleep for a few hours with my head next to the toilet. I wouldn't talk to him.

I was not killed. One day it was over. Somebody signed the papers. Now it is me in the lunchroom and the rain tapping on the windows.

Maria disappeared three days ago. I call Edison Park and ask for Justin. They hang up on me. My classes go well, move smoothly. In English class we write poems and the teacher tells me I have a knack for putting words together. I tell her I will be a famous poet, incredibly famous. People will love me.

I miss Maria. I feel lonely. I miss her. I miss her and Tanya and now they are both gone. It isn't fair. In science we grind up pills and make small experiments. The science teacher tells me that in the evening he peddles around on an old three-speed bicycle for hours. He tells me his wife is cheating on him with the neighbor. How horrible, when you are abandoned, destroyed, by someone so close. The science teacher confides in me. I am a good student now. Teachers confide in their good students. We grind up pills. The work is not hard and I am smarter than most of the kids here. They had little chance to begin with, but once they were put in the homes they had no chance at all.

At home we sit around the table for dinner. The food looks like plastic. Tracy sits at the top of the table. "So you're making good," she says shoveling a forkful of mashed potatoes into her mouth. I nod my head and pick at my food. "Trying to rise above yourself?"

I don't answer. Something dark is passing across her face. "Just don't get too big for your britches."

I push my plate away, lean back in my chair.

"You think you're better than everyone else."

"Everyone?" I ask her.

"You think you're better than the people you live with. The people in your school."

"I do," I tell her. "I definitely do. I think if anyone can get out of here and do OK, it is me."

"That's disgusting."

Ant and Jonathan and Phillip and Eric stare into their plates.

At night I read books and smoke cigarettes. The streets are calling me. I hear Chicago whispering for me. I hear my friends on the streets of Chicago.

If Chicago were mountains we could ski the buildings and hide behind rocks and fir trees. We could live along streams, live in tents. Instead of pimps there would be bears. The homeless could walk on snowshoes tracking for lost cities, rafting down rushing waters between shelter and day beds. There would never be a group home in the wilderness, no need for fires. State Street would be a hiking path, the Dan Ryan Freeway a rushing river blue and sparkling. If Chicago were mountains they would bulldoze the trees and fill the valley with cement. Angry steak palaces and storefront churches would be built atop the peaks. The city would rise again.

I prepare to set out into the Chicago wilderness. I run in the mornings before school. In the evenings I do sit-ups and push-ups. I don't eat candy. I don't eat fried foods. I go to school but I don't talk to anyone. I do my classwork.

The days and weeks pass quickly, quietly, and alone. I have started to grow a beard. Thin wispy hairs grow from my face. Starla wants to know what's wrong. "You're loosing weight Paul. You're looking old."

"It doesn't matter. Next year I'm going to worry about that. How's your boyfriend?"

"We're set to be married."

"That's good."

"Would you like to have a cigarette?"

"I'm not smoking." She looks at me oddly. "I'm in training," I tell her. I have to tell her. She's the only person left that I talk to. She may be the only person left in the whole world.

I follow her into the smoking room and she lights a cigarette for herself. She seems innocent when she smokes. Starla is older than me by ten years. Starla has clear skin and a long mouth with a tendency to smile. Starla sits on the windowsill and folds her hands over her knees. I want to have sex with her like I want to have sex with every woman I've ever seen, even big fat Tracy. But I don't care. I want to tell her everything.

"OK Paul," she says finally. "Tell me about your mission."

I exhale. I feel like I have been holding my breath forever. The breath leaves me for a long time and then I start rambling, telling Starla everything I can. "I am going to get straight A's this semester. They are going to let me go to the normal high school full time."

"Good for you."

"You wouldn't rat me out, would you?"

"Of course not."

"You wouldn't tell on me. You wouldn't get me in trouble. Because I have a hard time trusting people. And I want to tell you something, but it's very secret. It's private."

"I won't tell."

"After the semester," my throat dries up all of a sudden. Can I trust her? I get up, grab a glass of water, come back. She's still sitting there in long black pants and a long-sleeved white shirt. "After the semester there is two weeks before school starts again. It takes fourteen days to be staffed out. You know what I mean?"

"Go on."

"There are people missing. I have to find them. I can leave for two weeks and not be staffed out."

"Why do you feel you have to find them?" She settles into her social worker role. I hate that.

"Why do you stay with a man who ignores you?"

"He doesn't ignore me, Paul."

"I think he does."

"You'd probably like him if you got to know him."

"Don't count on it," I tell her. "I'm not so forgiving."

"And the world may not forgive you either."

"Look, I have to find them. I made some promises."

"You're no older than they are, Paul. You have to realize when to let go."

I scratch at my head. "I can't afford to let them go."

"But what if you find them? What then?

"Shit. I don't know."

People are missing and the winter is coming in. People are missing in the city. Perhaps they have left. Maybe Justin and Maria built those electric go-carts we used to fantasize about and drove away to some small town. Maybe Tanya was placed in a girls' jail downstate. I don't think so. I feel that she escaped. I feel it in my bones. The lonelier I feel the more I miss Maria, the more I miss Tanya.

I stuff socks, shirts, a pair of jeans into my backpack. I put in a notebook. Ant sleeps like a baby under his red and black flannel blanket. The morning is dusky, the windowpane cold. I rub my hands on my jeans. Ant and I haven't talked much recently. Starla told me his parents are thinking of taking him back. Wonderful of them. Little late though.

I walk down the stairs quietly. Tracy sleeps in her room. She never brings home a man. Nobody knows where she goes on the weekend. I do not care if she sleeps with other women. I fantasize about it. I fantasize about her tying me up, lying on top of me, smothering me so I can't breathe. I fantasize about her and I hate myself for it. Still, I do it all the time. I wish I didn't fantasize about big fat Tracy.

School ended yesterday. Thanksgiving is in a week. Then we go back for two weeks of activity, dodge ball, painting, group therapy. Nothing's graded. Then Christmas, New Year's, then the new school semester. They told me my file at Mather will read "behavior disorder." I told them I am a normal kid. But I am a ward of the court. Nobody believes a ward of the court.

The morning air is cold. Some of the streetlights are still on. A couple of old cars pass me, people are going to work. It is early and most of the city still sleeps. Shaka waves at me from the back of the Alston truck. He is bundled in a thick jacket, gloves, a scarf. I knew it would be cold on the truck.

By the time I get to Mather the sun has risen behind the school. It lights the grass on the field. I hum to myself. I have thirteen days to get back, or I get staffed out. I lose everything. If I do not get back I return to sleeping on rooftops, broom closets, hallways and boiler rooms on cold nights. A fresh piece of graffiti stains the dull Plexiglas windows. Mather is a large, pale blue, one-story structure. It looks like a fort, or some criminal hideout. The graffiti reads, "I Love You Dan."

There are trails stretching from it, running out into the street. I smell the paint but it is dry, must have been done last night. It was not there the day before. An elaborate message from a broken heart. A cassette tape lies by the door to the school, cracked in half. A confession? Who loves Dan? Who the fuck is Dan and what did he do to deserve this glorious homage? The letters start near the sidewalk, cover five windows. It is enormous. "I Love You Dan." It is beautiful. I want that. I want someone to write on the side of the Sears Tower, a note for the entire city of Chicago, for every man in a suit and every woman in a skirt. One hundred and thirty stories high, "I Love You Paul." That would be great.

I follow the paint trail. I walk along to Kimball. The sun is out and I feel it in my hair. A mirror in a storefront shows my face as I walk past. I hear a radio playing from a second-story apartment, *Where have all the good times gone?*

The winter is here and I am cold. Chicago has two seasons, ridiculous heat and freezing cold. I take buses across the city. I hang out for a while with the homeless kids at Rolling Stone Records on Harlem and Irving. Some of them remember me, some of them do not. Some of them have written "Ride The Lightning" for the new Metallica album on the back of their clothes.

I hang out in the parking lot near the large pink windows. Maria and Justin have not been here, ever. Tanya and I trampled through here, running away from Reed.

The homeless kids still hang out at this record store in torn blue jackets with cotton-lined hoods. I stand by them until one of them says to me, "Want to get high?" I nod and a pipe is passed to me. They show me where they crash down by the river. They sleep in patches of dirt. "You're welcome to hang out." I accept their offer. They have nabbed boxes from clothing stores and we all make two cardboard houses. I hang out for a day. We talk about life on the streets. We talk about our skills. One of the kids tells me he is an expert couch mover. He says his dad was a mover for thirty years. People that don't know anything always try to convince me that what they do know is worth something. Another one tells me he can start a fire without matches, while it's raining. A third tells me he took thirty hits of acid and tripped for three days. "It's true," someone confirms. "He licked the bag."

My time limit hangs over my head, a drop of frost in the trees. I have thirteen days. I have an agenda, people I need to see. I hang out, lying in the cold dirt, remembering why it sucks to be homeless. I have places to go. I have to retrace my steps.

I climb the fence of Reed. It is hard to see the fences of Reed; the eye misses them. It is the same in the day or in the night. Reed is hard to see. The fences are covered in grass and trees. The compound itself is practically below ground level. It is like an enormous trench one mile square. I slip getting over and cut my hand. I walk through the frost-covered field. The back wards are empty, silent. The back wards have a certain mystical feel to them. The only sound is my feet on the field. Rolling Stones Records and Labau Woods are just a half-mile away but Reed is in another world. From neither place can you see the other. Since I have been away I have not informed anyone of its existence, of Reed's existence, the adolescent center, the back wards. Somewhere in my own core I have denied it.

I come towards The Henry Horner Children's Adolescent Center. As I get closer I can make out the wire mesh on the windows. It's silly but I worry that at any moment some ogre is going to burst out of the doors and drag me back in. I worry that Tanya is inside, that she came here looking for something and the ogre pulled her inside by the ankles. I step carefully around the periphery trying to peer inside.

Molly seduced me into submission. Molly said she would adopt me, but I ran away. I locate her office, closest to the exit; the light is off. I hide behind a tree, and I wait.

After awhile the light goes on. I see her walk into the room followed by a patient. They talk for a bit. I move closer to the window, I know they can't see me. I try to pick up on her posture. I watch for how she crosses her legs. I masturbate watching her talk to this boy. I remember the smell of her dress.

I wait for hours. More boys. Every time she takes one back to the wards she brings a different one into her office. I look for patterns. She doesn't know I can see her. I can see Molly, her blond hair. I masturbate six times. I masturbate watching her sit in her chair, watching her cross and uncross her legs. The clocks tick on walls; the clouds move across the sky. I should never have had to come here. No one should ever come back here. When you lose something, the only way to find it is to retrace your steps, to go back to all the places you were, find where it fell out of your pockets, like looking for a key. I am retracing my steps. I am trying to find what I lost. It must be here, somewhere. But no one should ever have to come back to a place like this, with locked doors and wire on the windows, sadistic social workers, time out rooms, Thorazine and Kool-Aid, an adolescent mental health facility. This place needs to be forgotten and if enough people can forget it together then maybe it will no longer be here and in its place they will develop homes, build skyscrapers or giant factories. Anything. Anything would be better than this.

For a while she takes a break, leans back in her chair and reads someone's file. I lie down in the frostbitten grass exhausted. This takes about an hour before she puts down the file, leaves, and returns with another boy.

This time it is different. She leads the boy into the room by the hand. What is he in there for? Suicide? Assaulting his parents? The boy seems nervous, more nervous than the other ones. He has short, dark spiky hair. He starts talking, she leans in closer. Everything is different, the angle of her body, where her knees are, where she rests her fingers. I see memories. Then they kiss. Their knees touch, her hand is on his hand. They kiss for what seems like a long, long time. They are kissing. She is kissing him. His hand is lightly brushing her breast.

Finally she pulls away. The boy moves towards her and she puts her hand up to stop him. There is a large rock in the dirt and I throw it as hard as I can at the window. It hits the screen, denting it forward, crumbling along the ridges of concrete, making an enormous sound, like a bomb. They both turn and look in the direction it came from. I run as fast as I can away though the fields, past the empty back wards. I do not want to be dragged back inside. They will never let me out this time. I don't want anyone to grab my ankles. I swing over the fence and drop back down onto the street, trying to inhale and breathe.

Chicago is brutal in the winter. People die from frostbite. People stay in their homes next to hot air radiators. This winter has not gotten that bad yet, but it will. In the winter Chicago is an angry god. The winter I was homeless I would break into boiler rooms to keep warm, hang out in laundromats in the early morning. That was a rough winter. That was my roughest winter. When the state finally nabbed me sleeping in the hallway bleeding they did not believe my story. They did not believe I did not know where my parents lived. I lie sometimes but I was not lying then. That was a cold winter, the coldest ever. I am reverting to my old tricks.

I sit next to a boiler in the bottom of a three flat. I know I have to leave early, to avoid the adults. When you are a kid on the run you always want to avoid adults. The adults want to put you in cages, thwart your plans. The adults molest you, fondle you, cheat you out of everything you have. They are like lions in the jungle and the children are raw slabs of meat left out for them to devour.

I count out my money, close to thirty dollars. I get as close to the heater as I can but I am still shaking. The Chicago winter is getting into my bones. I open the package of hot dogs I bought, put one inside a slice of bread. I take a bite then lose my appetite. This is pathetic.

When I was a homeless kid other kids would feel sorry for me. None of them could take me home. But they would buy me hot dogs at a place called Gilly's. I was hungry but I hated when people felt sorry for me. Then I got angry at my father. Blamed him for my being there. If he had looked half as hard for me as I am looking for Maria and Justin and Tanya he would have found me. I would not have gone with him though, and maybe he knew that and that is why he did not look.

I pull out my journal and write a few lines. My father crossed a line, I was an unforgiving child. I write in my journal, "I forgive you." One day I am going to let him know I forgive him. He probably doesn't need it. He probably doesn't know that he did something wrong. Still, I will slip him the note, stick it under his door. I sleep and I hear the soft flame from the boiler.

Days pass. I comb the city, I move at night. More days pass. Evenings are giant neon crosses filled with train sounds, the hiss of spray paint cans, mice, rats and felt-tip markers. The train pulls into the station. The snow falls softly and I hear a pair of dice smack the street. A single light is on in the back of the train station, dim and yellow. My feet crunch the snow. The tiny flakes die beneath my feet.

The heating lamp hangs unlit. Painful memories spring to my eyelids. Laying in the corner, face buried in my own puke, the creatures came out of the wooden slats, sprung from the back fence. I touch my neck where my mother's silver necklace hung. I had given her a silver dollar on a chain when I was eight. When she died I got it back. The streets took it from me the way they took everything else.

Beyond the black of the night and the white of the snow, Washington Park spreads before the station like spilled oil, like a giant pool.

I tramp slowly the stairs, the cigarette butts. I pass two men waiting at the bottom of the stairs. I am a shadow. Across 55th, a slab of concrete in front of two rocks, sheets of mortar, a green bar closed forever with boarded-up windows. Here you can hide. The flashing blue lights will never come here. The shadows whisper danger. Every black corner is another country, with different rules. I have descended back into the streets of anarchy, back into the Robert Taylor Homes.

A trash can bangs to the ground, then a gunshot. "Psst," a whisper, a dark face in the doorway. "Come here." I step up to the door. "Have a drink with me." He hands me a bottle and I take a pull. "What are you doing out, whitey?"

"I'm looking for people."

"You ain't gonna find them here."

"I know." I pull some more on the bottle. I lean against the wall, slide down to the floor, rest my head. We sit across from one another, two sides of the same lie.

"If you lookin' to find someone you can't go looking at the end of the world."

"I thought I'd get some information."

"You better call the phone company."

I let my eyes close. I'm running out of time. It's been eight days.

On the fourteenth day it will have been too long, I will never be able to go back. The doors will close forever.

I feel the man's bony fingers on my shin. "You better call the phone company," he says and laughs to himself.

In the morning the sun falls on the snow. I look at the man across from me, passed out, bottle in his hand. My fingers trace my own features, the whiskers on my chin, the skin of my cheeks.

I gather myself together and step out the door. The world smells like fresh, cold air mixed with trash. I track down 55th with my backpack. The projects dominate the skyline, the Robert Taylor Homes are in everything you see. They are so immense they fill the cracks left between smaller buildings. They are at the back of every vacant lot. I do not know how many buildings make up the Robert Taylor Homes, but it must be at least a hundred, each one a half-block square and thirty stories into the sky. People are out, walking the streets, standing in doorways. They are wrapped in blankets, Salvation Army scarves, torn boots. People lived here once, differently from now, before they built these enormous projects.

I trip over a curb and land on broken glass. I pass a white trailer with purple graffiti. Rocks in the cuts in my hands sting me. The Vice Lords populate this entranceway, guard Willie's thick steel door. My old roommate, Cateyes, is on the end of them, two teardrops tattooed on his face. Cateyes stares at me. They stare at me as a group, I feel the breath behind me.

"What's in your bag?" he asks me.

"Some clothes. A notebook." The sun that's out is not a friendly one. The snow doesn't melt. It's hard to see. "I have to see Willie."

"You got an appointment?"

"What are you, his secretary?"

More time passes. I say, "Tell him it's Paul. Tell him I'll give him everything I have."

I sit down on the steps with the Vice Lords. They are not much different from the kids that tripped me on 55th, just a few years older. The worst thing about poverty is the boredom. They are kids without toys. There is nothing for them to do. They hang here day in and day out. They are criminals with no one to rob, mechanics without tools. We all sit on the steps, the novelty of a new face disappearing.

"Go on in," he tells me.

This room is well lit. Thick wooden shelves line the walls filled with books. Willie sits at his chessboard in the center of the room and smiles when he sees me. He motions for me to take a seat at the other side. He pushes a pawn. He will play white. I will play black. I push my queen's pawn only one space. French opening. I have to be careful, I never know what Willie is thinking. He is unpredictable. He always tricks me.

"Paul," he says. "Nobody comes back here. Nobody gets out and then comes back. It's like eating food you already know is poisoned. Didn't anybody teach you any better than that?" He shows me his large white teeth and pushes his queen's pawn a space. A very conservative opening. "You have to stop running away. It is important to stay in one place, to gather a base, to get to know people."

The walls in Willie's office seem thick, the musicians in the pictures tasteful. From this room he controls a small portion of the Robert Taylor Homes. He is one feudal lord appointed by an outside source. The Vice Lords in front of the door are his soldiers, his troops, police force, because the police never come in here. Where no rules are written unwritten law arises to take their place. Unwritten law is difficult to learn, easy to change. The society is in a constant state of upheaval. Willie knows that at any time he could be just another teardrop under an eye and takes necessary measures to hold onto his office.

"I'm looking for some people." I stroke the board. Prepare to move my king's pawn. Willie looks at his pawns, pretending to think, but he already knows what he is going to do. The air in the room is heavy, feels like we are in a cave.

"Why do you think I would know where they are?"

I shrug my shoulders. I push my king's pawn two, opening up, a traditional black response. "I ran away from a mental hospital with a girl, Tanya. The police found us and took her back, locked her away. Then I fell in love with a girl named Maria and she ran off with my friend Justin."

"You want my advice?" I nod. "Don't fall in love," he says. We both laugh. I open up my queen's side with my bishop's pawn. He attacks me with his queen's bishop. "You're just a kid, Paul. How old are you."

"I turned sixteen a week ago."

"You're just a kid."

"Yeah, well you're just a criminal whose power is derived as a parole officer and a drug counselor. You get your power from the state and they don't want to know what you do with it."

Willie descends on my pawn with his bishop, tucks it into his hand with his pinky finger and places it on the corner of the table. "Look at how young you are." He brushes his fingers along my cheeks. "You're shaking."

"So. I feel cold."

"Let me tell you something, Paul." He reclines in his chair. I stare at the board. I can't see a way to win. My position is already lost. "You will never find that girl, Tanya. Once they take a person like that away you can never find them again. Your other friends, maybe you can find them if you look long enough. But what then? Either she's walking the streets and he's her pimp or they're both strung out on junk, sleeping in some crack apartment. There are only so many endings to a given story. Once you find them, what do you do? Nothing, you turn around and go home. There's nothing you can do."

"You can't help a group home kid?" I don't bother to move any more pieces. "I don't think I'll come back here again, Willie. I'm afraid that if I came back here again I'd find your head on a stick."

Willie smiles broadly. Willie has thick, purple lips. "I think that's a strong decision on your part," he says. We sit still, relaxed. "What if I gave you your pawn back, Paul. What if you move your knight first, try to firm up your center position and we took it from there."

"You'd still trick me somehow." I lean back, examine the board. "Thanks for keeping me alive when I was here."

"Nobody else knew how to play chess." We sit for as long as is appropriate then I get up to leave and Willie walks me to the door. Outside the Vice Lords huddle under a cold sun. Willie stands in the doorway and the Vice Lords part for me, let me through, all of them looking away, Willie's eyes burning into my back. None of the Vice Lords look at me as I walk away.

The juvenile hall is located at 1100 South Hamilton, six stories high, two more stories deep, two blocks from Little Italy, two blocks from the University of Illinois, and two blocks away from the end of the line. I walk to the metal detector. I have nothing in my pockets. In front of me the juvenile courts, up the stairs the jail. A concrete statue stands in the middle of the floor depicting a man pushing a boulder. A guard passes, gives me a look. A lady, eyes wide with crack and hair sticking up to the ceiling walks by dragging a little girl by the wrist. The little girl is a victim of the Family First policy pushed by The Department of Children and Family Services. The stairs lead up to the cells. The hallways lead to the courtrooms, rows of them. But children are not allowed in the courts. The kids have to sit on the benches outside while their cases are heard inside and the DCFS workers and the judge and the Guardian Ad Litem make the decisions that will determine their future. If they ever let us speak in court they would hear some crazy things. The whole building would probably come down. Children and parents are everywhere. The court is crowded. They sit on benches or lean against the walls.

I walk up the stairs to the entrance to the jail. A beautiful Spanish woman sits at the desk and reminds me of Maria, except with her legs crossed higher and with cleaner teeth. "I don't suppose you could tell me who is inside?" I ask.

"Of course not," she says. I wonder if she is sleeping with any of the inmates. What a prize that would be.

"How about if I gave you ten dollars?"

"You better watch it kid or you'll end up inside yourself. You look like you've already been inside."

"I'm looking for Tanya. I promised I would take care of her." The lady shuffles papers, turns away. I hate being ignored. I exhale. "Look, I really need to see Tanya. She's been counting on me."

"I'm too busy. And anyway, I can't tell you who is inside. There are laws against that. If she did anything serious she's not here because we only take kids with short sentences."

"Where do they put the kids who kill their parents?"

"Well," she says without looking up, twirling a pencil over her fingers. "Perhaps a maximum security treatment facility like ISBY. Or, they could go to the long-term facility in St. Charles. If they're tried as adults they could be in Joliet or Marion."

"You can't try someone as an adult for killing their parents. Adults don't kill parents, only children kill parents." I'm speaking in Tanya's defense. Trying to win her release.

The lady looks up from her desk. "What's your name?"

"Paul."

"Goodbye, Paul."

I go down into the basement where there is a cafeteria. I buy a hot chocolate from the vending machine and sit at a brown linoleum table watching the guards come in holding their belts, guns and sticks hanging off them like laundry on a line. They buy instant coffee, candy bars, mustard pretzels. I gather my wits and head out to Maxwell and Halsted.

Maxwell and Halsted is a colorful place. People hawk dirty movies and fake gold chains. They sell Polish sausages from steaming shacks coated in grilled onions and mustard with thick french fries and strawberry sodas. Old men play guitar in front of trashcan fires. It is like an oasis of blight surrounded by empty buildings. It knocks on the edge of the University as well as the projects. Highways cross and circle around it. Men stand three to a circle around burning trashcans. Jewtown they call it, but there are no Jews here.

In a back alley a large sign proclaims, "The Maxworks." An empty bus sits in the lot painted in fading psychedelic colors. Justin and I came here on our way to hitchhike out West. Hippies were living in this building. They let us stay with them. They said it was a commune. The hippies are all gone now. They gave us acid and Justin had sex with one of the girls. It wasn't that long ago. Three years now. The hippies were mostly in their forties reminiscing about the good old days, the days of the revolution and how the Maxworks was going to change it all around. The building is like a book with all the pages torn out. Around the bus sit pieces of wire and cable, strips of fabric.

I knock on the door; there is no answer. There is no bell, no electricity in the abandoned building. So many buildings stand like this in Chicago. Homeless palaces. I step inside and there is a hallway. The beams are exposed through broken plaster; a mouse scurries down the hall. Nails stick from the walls. I walk the stairs and the second floor houses a row of what used to be apartments. There is a large opening with an old wooden bookshelf bolted into the hallway. A few dusty books still lie on a shelf. The building is cold and my breath forms clouds over my face.

I push the door open. Justin sits on a bed, a thin mattress on an old steel spring. Maria stands away by a window. She is not the pretty girl I met one spring in hot pink and cheap fashion earrings. She doesn't look like an unopened piece of candy. More like an empty wrapper. Under her eyes are large black pools, as if she had never slept a day in her life.

Justin looks up at me, his long hair covering most of his face. Aside from the bed the room is bare, no books, papers, dirty clothes, board games, appliances. No dishes, soaps, cups, pots, pans, posters, paintings, records, or radios.

"So," I say. "You want to go grab a soda?" It's cold as fuck outside but this room is not so cold. I wonder where the heat is coming from. I spent a Chicago winter homeless when Justin and I first ran away. I hope they don't lose this space.

"What are you doing here?" Justin asks.

"I didn't want to lose touch. I thought if you guys got married I could stand up at your wedding." I bite the inside of my lip.

"I didn't think I'd see you again," Maria says.

"I've been looking for you guys for twelve days."

"There's another room down the hall," Justin says. "You can stay if you want." He says it like he doesn't care one way or the other.

"I can't. I have to get back or I'll get staffed out. You know, lose my big chance."

"What big chance is that?" Justin says.

"I don't know what big chance. You know, Campbell House is a pretty soft home. And I'll be going to a normal high school. I could go to college."

"And then what?"

"Oh, you know. Join society, make some money. Maybe build a treatment center for FUCKED UP people like you."

Maria touches my arm. This room is so naked it is unbearable. It is the loneliest place on the farthest edge of the world. I pull Maria towards me impulsively. I hold her in my arms but she is limp, she won't give off any warmth. It's like hugging a piece of ice. I run my fingers through her hair. Justin stares down at the floor. Between the three of us he's the only one that's good looking. I think he'll be good looking forever, all the way through, until he dies, which will almost certainly be fairly soon.

I let go of Maria. I am afraid if I hold her too tightly I will crush her.

"Nobody can tell us what to do here," Justin says.

"That's true," I concede. "You will always be the last to leave the party. Two Answers," I say to Maria.

"I am never going back," she replies. "Things will never be OK."

"You sure have gotten thin," I say to Maria and she smiles a little. I don't know what else to say. I wish I had brought a deck of cards or something. I guess I never really expected to find them. I brush Maria's fingers. "What do you guys do here? Aren't you bored? Do you play games?"

"Same things you do," Justin says.

"Oh. Homework?"

"When did you become such a nerd?"

"This is insanity. You guys can't survive here." I look to Maria.

"You can't be normal," Justin sneers under his head full of long black hair. I look over at him. It is warm in here. I could stay here, stay warm, at least for a few days. I walked through a fire for this. I walked through a fire and found a burned down building.

"Paul..." Maria says.

"Yes?" I look to her. I look to her drawn skin, her sunken cheeks.

"I hope you find what you're looking for. I hope everything turns out OK for you."

I reach out to Maria's cheek. She doesn't flinch, no movement. "You don't have to stay here," I tell her. "Let's go back."

"Don't worry. Justin will look out for me."

"I'll look out for her."

"We made a commitment to each other."

When Maria mentions commitment I think of Tanya. Maria goes over to the mattress and sits down next to Justin. I put my bag down and sit with my back against the wall for a few hours. Then I get up to leave. I close the door behind me, listen for the silence. Nothing.

The clock on the wall of Neon Street Shelter for Homeless Children reads 8:30 a.m. The neon shelter holds court over Belmont Avenue. Kids sleep under wrinkled blankets on either side of me. The room is an orchestra of wheezing and tiny breaths, of fingers scuttling the floor, scouring for loose change, searching out loose change like a bird forages for tiny crumbs of bread. Across from me large windows stare out onto Belmont Avenue and the Belmont train station.

It's Sunday morning, the thirteenth day. A few passengers are huddled under thick jackets on the train station's wooden planks. Big flakes of snow have just begun to fall from the sky. They won't stop falling now for four months. That's the way Chicago winters are, dry and unforgiving, lit by hot air radiators, punctuated with crime.

I was not sure I was going to make it. Last night, in a dream, Starla bent over me. I crawled up inside her, curled up like a baby. I felt warm, and then suffocated. Then Starla kissed me goodbye. But today she will welcome me back. It is the thirteenth day and I am going to go home to Campbell House and a new school. It was warm in that building with Maria and Justin. For a moment I thought about staying, not with them, just with the streets.

I sit up in my bed and see a boy scamper away in the space between the bunks. My bag is checked in the other room, my notebook, my clothes, so I am safe. Big fluffy flakes of snow powder the Chicago wilderness, build up on rails, on top of buildings. The snow continues to fall until the sidewalks are buried, the cars can no longer move. The people disappear beneath the snow, the plastic signs outside of doorways vanish. It snows so long and so much that soon even the Robert Taylor Homes are covered beneath it, the Sears Tower, and now, Chicago is mountains, and I set myself to journey into the wilderness.

5. NINE MONTHS

Group homes are funny places. There are a lot of ways to end up in a group home. Girls get picked up for prostitution. Boys get picked up for stabbing people with ice picks, cooking crack, and raping their sisters. Girls get picked up for being left behind. Boys get left behind. Girls get adopted, dropped off, and adopted again. If someone's parent refuses to pick him up when he is scheduled to be released from the Juvenile Hall, then the child is put into a group home and the state takes custody. Other kids have no parents and cannot be adopted on account of some personality flaw, behavioral disorder. Some kids are put in foster homes and then the foster parents realize how fucked up they are and give them back to the state. You only get one chance. Some kids are pulled away from parents deemed unsuitable, and tossed in group homes. Parents are tried and convicted of abuse and neglect. The state takes custody, the child is branded Property of the Department of Children and Family Services, State of Illinois. The child is put in a group home. The one thing every group home kid has in common is at some point they were ignored by someone. Every group home is different. Some have sports teams. Some are out in the woods five miles from the nearest hitchhiking road. Many line the housing projects and the least valuable pieces of land in the nation's biggest cities. The worst group homes are fish tanks, gladiator arenas, thirty to a room, make friends fast, hope for the best. In the worst group homes we just kill each other quickly. The state doesn't want to know, we do not want to tell. In the better group homes there is a modicum of supervision and, more importantly, there are better kids with shorter records. Group homes are funny places. They are located in regular houses, in brick institutional structures. They are tent cities. They are invisible. They are in the suburbs, they are in the ghetto, they are in everything in-between. Some group homes maintain control with locked rooms and Thorazine. Other group homes leave you to get your hair pulled out in clumps by crazed madmen. Some group homes give you a dollar for every day you go to school. They are built, then left alone. They are pre-programmed for destruction. You pick up your own pieces. You do your best.

Nine months ago a girl disappeared from a girls' group home on Rosemont Avenue and fell off the side of the earth. She landed on Maxwell Street in a naked apartment with a strung-out drug addict. Nine months has brought rains and sun and traffic to the city. She gave up. She decided not to exist. She looked me dead in the eye and told me she was broken. She told me things would never be OK. She also told me I was looking for something else. I knew she was right. She took a step into the mouth of the world and the world swallowed her whole. Nine months is a long time. Anything can happen in nine months. A baby can be born. The seasons can change three times.

"Smoke?"

"Thanks."

Ant and I walk down California Avenue. Winter has come and gone, has taken the snow. Summer has passed, again. Ant has gone with the winter and returned by summer's end. His parents took him back, carted him off to some school in the suburbs for problem children. Here he is again, nine months later, and we are walking to school. He checks his reflection in windows, stops and combs his long honey-colored hair. He holds his hair to the wind so it doesn't lose its place. My own hair has grown out around my head like a blonde curly Afro, thick and dry. Tracy keeps telling me to get it cut but I won't. I have a complex about it. We pass a colorful garage not yet open for business. The door to the garage is painted a bright blue, like a sky with the hours of operation in big yellow letters, a bright blue sky. And here, now, I walk along with Ant in the early fall morning. I love a quiet morning. The businesses are mostly closed. Storefront tailors still have bars across the windows. There are no alarms sounding, just people driving to work somewhere.

Cars pass by on California Avenue, then buses.

"What time is it?"

"8:30."

We don't say much. Ant and I share a room, there's not much left to say in the mornings. We know each other pretty well. On Devon there is a new bank with a big blue heading. It is just cold enough that we keep our hands in our pockets as we pass the bank. Across the street from the bank there is a small diner. Painters, construction workers, truck drivers, plumbers, and movers sit on stools at a bar in faded jeans covered in sawdust, chalk and paint and eat cereal and drink coffee. We pass a video store. We pass what used to be Pita House but is now an empty storefront. Someone spray painted, "Go Home You Greek Bastard," on the window. It is all familiar. The colors do not stick out, the streets are not surprising. Even if this was all new and a wind was not blowing and it was not the first day of yet another school year. Even if it was so hot that we walked down California Avenue naked, it would still be a less than middle class neighborhood in Chicago filled with toilet cleaners, plumbers, three-flat apartment buildings, fast food restaurants. A smattering of uninteresting graffiti, a handful of gangs.

We pass the grammar school. We pass Glendale Avenue where we can see the girls' group home. The name of the home is 'Price' and sometimes we say, "Everybody pays at Price," and, "No Price is too low." It is just a three-story building. Boring as hell looking. Past that we come towards the gas station and behind that Wolfy's Hot Dogs with the grotesque plastic sign, an enormous beet-red hot dog stretching into the sky.

At the small red brick school we stop for a moment. A car pulls into a space in the alley. Ant hands me a cigarette and we both light up. I like the smell of a cigarette and clean air in the morning. Ant combs his hair a few times before putting his comb back in his pocket.

"Guess it's time," Ant says.

"Guess so."

At the door Ant rings the bell. A light goes on and a small hum sounds. He opens the door and goes inside.

I step on my cigarette and take a look into the sun, cross Peterson, walk through the playground, past the tennis courts, the basketball court, the park, through the doors, past a metal detector and a bulldog-faced security guard, past rows of dark green lockers; struggle through the crowd as a thousand adolescents bump and reach for their homerooms with elbows and rubber shoes, lockers rattle, doors open and shut in concert. Everyone is talking, some people yell, others whisper. I find the room I am supposed to be in and sit down just as a bell hollers across the school.

A short man with gray hair takes attendance. White T-shirts, black shirts with logos. One kid wears a black shirt with gold stripes: Latin King colors. Kids sit at desks with their eyes down, some of them hulking monsters. This is a junior class, third year Chicago public high school. Some of the kids in this room are too big for high school. Some of them are nineteen with big round shoulders and a few capped teeth. The room is overcrowded and on the verge of exploding.

The teacher doesn't notice. He takes attendance. He is small. In a war he would be the first to burn. He reads off the names. "Laronda, Tammy, Stephanie…" Girls with gelled-up hair and low-cut halter tops answer, "Yes, here. Hello, present. The one and only. What?" When it is over we all sit for a bit. Somebody laughs. Some of the boys wear blue jerseys with white numbers. Football players. I look for a power structure. How many gangs? How many football players? Somebody throws a ball, then a sheet of paper. Finally the teacher looks up and says, "OK, cut it the fuck out."

My first class is physics. The physics teacher has a pointy beard and resembles a bird. He tells us we need to get science notebooks. We have to buy our own. He says we are going to do experiments. I sit at a big wooden table with another boy and two girls. They know each other and ignore me.

"Did you know Jamie's got nickel bags?"

"Good?"

"Shit, I don't know. What you asking me for."

"I messed up this bitch this summer. I said, Pow, Pow. Bitch dropped like a bomb."

"Hell no."

"Did you hear about Peter?"

"What happened?"

"He was shot in front of Moscow at Night."

"Oh shit." The girl covers her mouth, the teacher looks up.

The teacher says, "You start with a basketful of water and you pour it on the ground. The water still exists, it is just somewhere else." The teacher wags his finger and paces in front of the board.

The classes continue. Each class is forty minutes long and then ten minutes to fight your way through the crowd to the next class. The other kids seem to glide easily through the turmoil. I get elbowed and kneed and bumped by backpacks and book bags. Between classes the lockers release a steady roar of green tin opening and slamming shut.

At lunch period I sit outside of the building chewing on a sandwich Tracy packed for me. The painting that used to be on this school, that some heartbroken girl had left, has been cleaned. "I love you Dan," but does she still have a broken heart? When they cleaned the paint were they back together or was it just a cleaner school? There were great big letters on the school that day.

Kids play on the basketball court. I sit at the curb of the rounded street that passes in front of Mather High. I take a couple of bites then I pitch my sandwich. A small group of boys turn the corner with guns and start shooting. The guns are just water pistols and they soak this kid while the kid is trying to cover himself and it seems innocent enough. Then one of them hits him in the stomach and another kicks his legs. The kid's wet body smacks onto the cement. The kid cries and they take the basketball away from him and he runs off crying somewhere and the others stand there with water pistols wondering what to do now. They do not want to play basketball. They look around, confused, trying to lock eyes with someone. One of them says, "I ain't no kid. I'm a man!" and thumps his chest hard with the back of his fist. They leave the ball and the ones that have been there resume playing as if nothing has happened, and I suppose nothing has.

In English the teacher is sitting on her desk lecturing and we are all looking at her legs when the loudspeaker opens. "Paul F——, please report to the office."

"That's me," I say.

The teacher stares at me down the bridge of her nose. I gather my books and put them in my backpack. The hallways are empty now. One kid runs down the end of the hall and then out of the door. Each room contains thirty or more kids waiting for a break. On the southern corridor there is a mural. A huge blue and gold dragon swimming through a sea of textbooks. I present myself to the office.

"I'm Mrs. Laticia."

"Nice to meet you," I say. Her hands are enormous.

"We need to make a schedule for you."

"For what?"

"We have extra sessions for all our LBD kids."

"What's that?"

"Learning/Behavior Disorder."

I squint my eyes and look at her. "That doesn't apply to me."

"It's on your record." Her hand rests on top of a manila envelope.

"I don't have one of those." Pause. "That's just because I'm a ward of the court."

We sit for a second. The front office is just a small room with two long wooden benches and small windows with bushes running the length and we're both standing. "At any rate we have no test for you. We need IOWA tests to place you in your classes. Haven't you ever been tested?"

"I've been tested but I don't think I've taken those tests."

"Can you stay after school tomorrow and do them?"

"Sure."

I meet Ant at a bench at the end of the park. He cuts at a piece of wood with his pocketknife. The buses and the cars coming home early from work pass us by. Ant pulls a candy bar from his pocket and offers it to me but I shake my head. I recognize some of the people passing from my classes.

"I'm tired of school," Ant says. "It's boring. It's just a bunch of retards."

"It is." We are on the corner of Mather Park and the sun is shining on both of us in different ways. Ant hides behind his sunglasses, I hide behind mine. I stick my tongue out and make a gargling sound with my tongue. "So what are you thinking?"

"I'm going to drop out. They'll never let me go to a normal school."

"You wouldn't like it. It's crowded."

"I'm not cut out for school."

"So you're gonna drop out?"

"Yeah."

"And do what?"

"I don't know. Do maintenance or something."

"You don't know how to fix anything."

"I could be a janitor."

"Don't janitors have to fix things?"

"Naah. They just walk around in the basement of buildings in overalls. They're like security in case somebody tries to steal your pipes or something."

I nod my head. It is fall. Falls in Chicago are full of forgiveness, softening the city for the winter. The fall is pleasant. I think of the fall as the mother, gentle, naked in a warm bed with long arms and comforting words. I smell the fall. Winter can be the father, screaming, spit flying off his lower lip, a storm inside a house, a room without a roof, the cheeks sliding off of his face into oblivion. In the spring they can make up and in the summer they can fuck like dogs.

"Sure, you could be a janitor. What would Tracy think?"

"Who cares."

"If you drop out of school they're going to kick you out of the home."

"Well, I'm not going to drop out just yet. I'm just thinking about it." Ant taps the wood. Across the street some Chinese kid is messing with the lock to a small sporting goods store. It looks like he's trying to rob the place. "Did you ever find Maria?"

"Yeah."

"I was just wondering."

"Last I saw Maria she was living in some abandoned building down on Maxwell Street." I don't mention Justin. I don't mention what I saw on the street, the overturned garbage cans, the fires, the men with jackets full of fake gold chains and porno movies. I can't mention it. I don't mention how empty the room was, how warm and how empty, and how skinny Maria was.

We walk down California. "So how's Larry and Breen," I ask him.

"They're good."

"They ever give you trouble?"

"No. We're friends." He lights up a cigarette and gives me one. I light it up. An egg thrown from a car lands in front of us and explodes in yellow yolk-filled streaks across the sidewalk. "You want to smoke some pot?"

"Sure."

We cut down an alley. Ant packs a tiny pipe and passes it to me. I suck down the smoke. I don't take too much because sometimes Ant gets a little weird about his pot. I kick a stone. The alley has a lot of broken glass and graffiti on the garage doors.

"My grandmother has cancer," he says. "They had to cut one of her breasts off."

"That's fucked up."

"Yeah. I was staying with her. My folks don't want me to come back to their place."

"How come?"

"I don't know. I think they wanted a kid with more ability. They're not too pleased with me. But I can't stay with my grandmother now because she has cancer. Though I guess she doesn't have it anymore. Now that they cut her breast off."

"That must look weird."

"You can't tell. She wears a fake one so when she wears a sweater it looks the same. It looks better." He takes a big hit off the pot, passes the pipe back to me. It is pretty good stuff. "She has a boyfriend."

"You're kidding."

"Serious man. Some old dude."

"I guess old dudes get lonely." I cough some smoke.

"Yeah," he says. "Old dudes get so lonely they start fucking chicks with only one tit." He giggles and I laugh some more. "That old bitch." A cruiser with blue horns comes down the alley towards us and Ant ditches the pipe behind a garbage can.

"What are you kids doing here?"

"Walking."

"Why don't you walk, then?"

"We are walking."

"Don't get smart kid. I'll knock your teeth out." The cop doesn't even get out of the car. Ant and I move along.

"That was pretty bold, Ant."

"What?"

"The way you ditched that pipe."

"You think so?"

"Absolutely."

"Let's go back and get it." We go around the block and back down the alley. The pig is gone.

"I've never been happy to see a cop," I say. "Ever."

Ant picks up the pipe. I am pleasantly stoned. We cut across the grammar school and take side streets. There is a private Catholic school on Washtenaw, St. Timothy's. "They all look the same." The children make me think of my little brother and sister, running in circles in some Catholic school. I sure would like to see them. God, it's been years since I left home.

"Paul?"

"What?"

"What are you doing?"

"Nothing. I'm just standing here. I'm just stoned." I rub my hands over my face. Ant looks at me and then confesses.

"I've been crying."

"What?"

"I've been crying," he tells me.

"Why? What about?"

"I don't know. It just comes over me and I start crying. That ever happen to you?"

"Yeah, back when I was in the mental hospital."

I feel pretty good and stoned. This is the first time Ant has ever seemed interesting to me. We sit on a bench on Devon across from the Devon Bank. We sit for a while and then there is a car crash. The same cop who bugged us earlier comes back and starts directing traffic around the crash. "What a fucking jerk," I say to Ant. "He's nothing but a stop sign."

We split the scene and continue down more side streets. The leaves are changing colors. In one window some fat guy gives his kid a haircut. "I don't get it," he tells me.

"Maybe there's something wrong with you, Ant."

"Maybe."

Tracy and Ant and Jonathan and Phillip and Eric and I sit around the dinner table. I can't eat. The food is dry. Sometimes I don't like food. "So, how do you like your new school?" Tracy asks. She dumps some peas and cold pasta on her plate. Phillip stares intently at his plate. He stopped talking. He hasn't spoken in three months.

"I'm not that hungry."

"Eat."

"The new school is crowded."

"Well it's where you wanted to be. Now you're there you don't like it." She shovels food into her mouth. The sun sets earlier in the fall. Out the windows it's getting dark. The table is long and has plenty of space to eat.

"They had me take an IOWA test today."

"What's that?" Jonathan asks.

"It's just a test. They ask you history questions and stuff. They also ask you vocabulary words and they give you words and ask you to define the relationship between the words."

"They're not supposed to give you tests without contacting us first," Tracy says.

"Every kid in the school has taken one. It's how they determine whether or not to put you in an honors class."

"I want to go to an honors class," Eric says. Eric is getting tall. He's twelve years old now. The other day he asked me if it was OK to masturbate. I told him he better learn how to read first.

"You just got there," Tracy says. "You don't need to be in honors classes."

I shrug my shoulders. She doesn't know shit. I can go to the administrators and have her overruled.

"Our school wasn't good enough for you."

"What you mean 'our school', white man?"

"Eat your food."

"I'm not hungry."

"Fine. Then don't eat. In fact, don't come back to this dinner table anymore. Feeding you is a waste. You think the whole world revolves around you." She gets up, grabs my plate and walks it into the kitchen loudly pouring the food into the trash bin.

"The sun sets in the West," I tell her. "Everyone knows that."

Charlie comes in shades of light blue across the afternoon entranceway. He is like a ballet dancer, a broken figurine. He is a light blue pair of sandals. He is the sound of traffic on the street. Skinny and in scuffed shoes, he shakes hands with Tracy while the rest of us look on pretending to be bored. Charlie doesn't look our way but Charlie has cold blue eyes. Charlie's caseworker talks with Tracy with one hand perched lightly on Charlie's thin shoulder. He looks my age. They show him his room. It's just off the kitchen with Eric. Tracy and the caseworker talk some more. Ant leaves. I sit with Eric and Jonathan writing in my school notebook. Tracy comes to us. "That's your new housemate, Charlie Mathews. I expect you'll be nice to him."

"Sure. Why wouldn't we be? Why would anybody ever not be nice? Nice of the stork to drop him off here." She looks like she is going to spit on me for a second but she doesn't.

I walk in on Charlie lying on his bed staring at the ceiling the same way I did when I first came here. "Looking for something?" I ask him.

"Just a little rest."

I nod and sit on the windowsill. Charlie's a skinny kid with faded denim. He stares into the ceiling. They say moving is the most stressful thing. I look at his skinny legs, they look longer than they really are. Thin arms folded behind his head, stringy blond hair falls over his eyebrows.

"Where'd you come from?" I ask him.

"The street. And I'll be back too."

"Lots of streets in this city."

"Mmm, miles of pavement."

Eric walks in. "Who said you could be in my room?" I ignore him. Eric rummages through a box crowded with cheap, broken dolls and puzzles with missing pieces.

"So just when you going back to those streets?"

"I guess I'll go tonight."

"You know there's a curfew here."

"So they've told me."

"I'll go with you," I tell him.

"Alright."

Charlie takes me to Addison and Broadway. Addison and Broadway is full of freaks. Cars prowl along the pavement, pock-marked men hover around neon pink bars. Some scowl when they pass us, others say hello. Girls walk Broadway Avenue past The Treasure Island. "Hello boys," they say. "Hello Charlie." The girls have husky voices and strong legs and most of them stretch past six feet in heels. Charlie wears the same jeans and a pale yellow dago-T covered by a thin ratty denim and keeps his hands in his pockets like he's cold and his eyes wide open, pulling the environment. He is sleepy, awake and aware. His hands in pockets give the impression of an angry child with a knife.

A girl stops. "This is Candy," Charlie tells me. "Candy, this is Paul."

"Do you want to get to know me better?"

I shake my head and she runs a long finger through my hair. "Boy, you need to cut that Afro." Her fingers twine my hair. "C'mon," she says. "Let's go over there." She nods towards a light brown building with a green dumpster in front and a chain-link fence running a passage between. She licks the top of my ear but I still say no. "What's wrong with your friend?" She says to Charlie. "Doesn't he like to have fun?"

"He knows what he wants," Charlie tells her looking down the avenue, waiting for his ship to come in. "See everything you wanted to see?"

"I'm just hanging out," I tell him. "Don't mind me."

"I won't."

A long black Lincoln pulls to a stop by the 7-11. Charlie walks past the white paper box *Chicago Tribune*, the yellow paper box *Chicago Sun Times*. Charlie gives me a look. In the night it's hard to make out his blue eyes before he climbs into the Lincoln and drives away.

The street is not empty but it is lost. People mill around, not many of them, but enough. They walk from one bar to another. They step behind trees for blowjobs, for hits from a pipe. The streets sell themselves but the money is circular. The streets pay themselves for their pavement. A bull with horns comes past. I climb on top of the newspaper box. The girls walk away. The cop shines his light on me. I cover my eyes from the brightness. The car passes with the rest of the traffic.

"Paul," Candy says. I turn around and she opens her shirt for me. I think about it for a second. Her breasts are perfected, like they were molded out of plastic. I sit perched on my box. "Don't you want to?" I don't reply. "C'mon Paul. You afraid I'll laugh? I won't laugh. I'll make you a man." Candy giggles and keeps on walking. Her see-through heels go Clack Clack Clack.

Minutes feel like hours. Some young rocker couples walk by hand in hand, earrings in their ears. Doors slam, flags hang from the lightposts. The Lincoln comes back and Charlie gets out in just his shirt and jeans and reaches back in to grab his jacket and closes the door in one motion. He approaches me smiling. It's a broken smile. He hands me five dollars. "Thanks for keeping watch for me," he says.

"Anytime," I tell him. We board the subway, try to get home and in the house without anyone noticing.

Charlie and I become friends. He walks with Ant and I to school in the morning. Charlie goes to school with Ant and I continue across the street to Mather's lawn.

Charlie sneaks out nearly every night and sometimes doesn't come home. Tracy never says anything. Sometimes I go with him and 'sit watch.' He always flips me a few bucks for my troubles but I don't do it for the money. Sometimes Candy brings guys back by the green dumpster and I look out for her and she gives me two bucks when she's done. Once I go over and watch the guy on his knees kissing her ass and jerking off onto the ground. Candy sees me watching and smiles for me. She turns around and takes out her enormous penis and the man takes it in his mouth. Candy does it for me, smiles for me, licks her lips for me. I walk back to my perch.

I smell Charlie when he walks the black streets, when it rains. When it rains the streets really shine. The streets suck in and return the glare of the streetlights. When it rains Charlie steps off the curb and I huddle beneath neon signs. Charlie steps in and out of the rain, comes and goes, leaves for days at a time. He moves between the raindrops while I keep my hands in my pockets. He leaves for three days and comes back and gives me five dollars for watching out. It's insane. I concentrate on my schoolwork. I try to leave Charlie to the streets. I can hear Charlie every morning because he sounds like a car pulling away.

• • •

The chess team meets every Tuesday after school in a small room towards the back of the school with a view of the parking lot. Most of the teachers are already gone and the cars with them. Most of the kids are gone too and with them the noise and the violence. Only the blue clad warriors running stonewall into pads remain in the front of the school. The football players stay long after everyone else has left.

Mr. Dell is a small man with big eyes and large gray eyebrows. He doesn't play chess. He looks suspicious when I show up and he sees the dagger tattooed on my left shoulder. He sees the tattoo and doesn't think I can play chess but I can play chess. I learned from Mr. Macy and Willie. Checkered mats are unrolled on the long brown tables with a tan satchel full of pieces next to each. The chess team is made up of five boards and two alternates for a total of seven kids counting myself. I play a couple of games. I am the second best player here, after some Russian kid named Alex Butterman. "Butterhead," I call him when I sit down to play against him. He glares at me but he is a skinny runt and nothing to be afraid of. Alex plays well, slams the pieces down when he moves, squirms in his chair, makes noises.

"You shouldn't make it so easy on me," he says in this thick Russian accent.

"I could choke you with two fingers," I tell him quietly.

"It is just chess," he says. "Not Ultimate Combat."

"You're going to play second board," Mr. Dell tells me. There is a girl on the team too. Her name is Jessica and she is tall and thin with black hair and big cheeks, a tiny button nose, large red lips, and skin the color of milk. Jessica wears a shirt with patches.

"I'm also a cheerleader," Jessica tells me. We sit down to play a game. I play white and she plays black and I hit the clock and push my pawn.

"That's kind of stupid," I say. I never have been very good with girls.

"No. It's good to be involved in things. I want to go to a good university."

"You should probably be in a private school then. Are your parents poor or something?" I ask her.

"No. Nothing like that." We push our pawns and bring our knights out. I like Jessica, she seems normal. She is pretty too. She pulls her queen out. "You think I can't play because I'm a girl."

I fork her king and her queen with my knight and take her queen off the board. "You play fourth board. That means you are better than three people here and not as good as three people here."

"Don't put so much faith in rankings," she tells me, and pushes a bishop towards center. It is too late. The damage is done. Five moves later I have won the game. She looks up from the mat. "I bet I am better than you at a lot of things," she decides. I shrug my shoulders.

"I'm not good at too many things so that should make it easy on you."

Mr. Dell puts his hand on Jessica's shoulder. "Who won?" he asks.

"I did." His hairy fingers sit on her shoulder like bugs. I stare at his fingers, the thick gray hair growing out just below the knuckles. Teachers are lecherous bastards. All the teachers want to fuck their students, want to keep their students after school and fuck their young students in the parking lots, in the teachers' lounge. His hand slides off her shoulder and he ambles down to the other end of the table.

"You know, it would have been better manners to let me tell him that you won," Jessica informs me.

"You must have a lot of time on your hands, to be so concerned with manners. Did you go to finishing school or something?"

"Are you in a hurry to get somewhere?" She asks me. We set up the board again. We push a lot of pawns. I am playing black. It is a slow, defensive game. She catches me napping and snaps up my queen's side bishop. "You think you're tough because you have a tattoo."

"Where I come from everyone has tattoos."

"Where do you come from, Mars?" She takes a series of pawns across my center. The board is demolished. A fucking nuclear war. Next time Mr. Dell comes around I let him know she won.

Mrs. Laticia put me in the honors English class. I should have known Jessica would be in the class too. It was obvious. All of my other classes are regular. She said next year I can take college preparatory classes. I should have known that Jessica would be here. I am sure that she is in every honors class. She sits next to some football player named Pete and I take the seat assigned to me on the other side of the room. Pete has a hard, sculpted face and blue eyes. He has big shoulders, a big nose and big lips. He wears a lot of gel in his hair and has the effect of being made out of plastic. The class is not as crowded as the other ones. Everyone is wearing slightly better clothes. I keep wondering why all of these kids are not in private schools. A lot of the kids are Asians, immigrants. Maybe we are all wards of the court. Maybe there's a dozen group homes in the neighborhood and we are the cream of the crop. Maybe every other house is a group home. We have a secret world. Secret tunnels connect all the group homes underground. The tunnels were built by the first wards of the state, our ancestors. Of course we were just apes back then, Neanderthal wards of the court. The tunnels are hidden now, forgotten. If we knew, we could take over, but we do not know. I like to think that we are all from group homes, and then Mrs. Roman calls on me.

"I didn't read the book. I didn't know I was going to be in this class."

"You'll have to read it by tomorrow." A couple of kids laugh. Pretty funny stuff.

After class I grab Jessica by the arm. "Hey."

"Hey yourself," she says. The football guy is with her. "This is Pete," she tells me.

I don't give a shit, I think to myself and then I say it. "I don't give a shit," I say. Then I stick my hand out. "Paul." He doesn't take my hand, just walks away. "I thought honors class was for smart kids."

"Pete is smart," Jessica tells me. "Smarter than you apparently."

"Why am I not smart?"

"Because you just picked a fight with someone you don't even know."

"I didn't pick a fight. I don't want to fight him. I'm not much of a fighter, to tell you the truth."

"No don't," I say. After school Pete punches me in the stomach and then the mouth and I go down pretty hard. Jessica intervenes on my behalf, and looking up from the grass I see Pete push her but then she grabs him again and pulls him away. A group of kids stand around me like witches and wizards and I wait for them to pile stones on my body or something but they don't. They don't care about me at all. They just walk away leaving me lying in the grass.

Ant smokes in front of the red brick school with Charlie, Breen, and Larry. The day is over for the social workers and the teachers and the fucked up retarded screwed up undone group home brats. "Hey guys," I say.

"What happened to your mouth?" Charlie asks. He touches my lower lip and I flinch away.

"I got beat up by some football player." I look over Larry and Breen.

"Because you got a big mouth," Larry says to me.

I shrug and run my hands through my hair. "Give me a cigarette." Ant hands me one out of his pack and lights it with his Zippo.

"You look fucked up," Breen says.

"Well, you know. That school across the street. They're barbarians. Bunch of meat-headed football players. They don't understand reason." We all smoke a bit.

"Put 'em in a home see how long they survive," Larry says. Geez his arms are huge.

"Damn right," I agree. This makes all five of us laugh. The group homes are just such funny places. "I sure was eager to get over there."

In English class Mrs. Roman asks me what happened to my mouth and I tell her I am tired of talking about it and I see Pete laugh a little in his seat and Jessica gives him an elbow in the ribs. This is not over. Mrs. Roman asks me if I have read the book. I say that I have. The book is *The Trial* by Franz Kafka. I start to talk about it. I can hear the silence. I can hear the class listening. I talk about Joseph K. I talk about the arrest and the priest stooped under the altar. I talk about lessons and sacrifices. I talk about truth and betrayal and climbing a stairway that never ends. No one says anything at all. I just keep talking about this book. I say I did not really understand the artist. I say I was on a street corner last night. I talk about how people get lost. I say it is like this girl Tanya I knew that I cannot find because she is hidden somewhere. Tanya was arrested at birth but never told her crime. I wonder about the tenements, but then I start to talk about the tenements that litter the city and the courts in the top of the building. I talk about just trying to understand, to grasp for one lousy second and how even that is not really enough because you forget too quickly. I talk about losing the most important things. I talk about taking more than the minimum, persecution, being chased, being woken up. I talk about courts, waiting to see a judge, never knowing who or where the law is and who is responsible for drawing the line. No one knows what I mean when I mention benches and security guards and coffee machines in the lower levels of courthouses. No one knows who I am talking about when I mention Willie and Willie's laws, his kingdom. So I go back to the parable: the man with the keys and the man who would not go in the door and died in front of it. I talk for fifteen minutes and nobody says anything, not a word. And when I am done everyone laughs.

Charlie spits his gum out and lights a cigarette, thinks better of it, throws it away, then lights another one. I lick my mouth. "This is boring," I tell him.

He points his finger up at me. He waits. I wait with him but I feel restless. I think even the darkness of the city can get boring. Not for Charlie I guess. He thinks about the money.

"I'm going to go home."

"What home?" He throws me his packet of cigarettes and I light one for myself and stuff the rest in my pocket. "You don't have a home. What are you going to do? Go back and fuck that fat bitch Tracy."

"Go do some homework."

"You're done with your homework. I saw you doing it already." Charlie smiles a crooked smile for me. But I'm bored, and as I'm thinking about Charlie I am also thinking about Jessica. My life revolves around school and the chess team and Charlie's street corner. Something has to give.

"Tell me about playing chess," Charlie says still looking towards the street.

"Well," I say. "Nobody's supposed to win because of a mistake. The idea is to force the opponent into a position where there is no right move. That's why position is so important. Most games are won or lost very early on. If two people are good and one gives up a pawn he will usually resign. You can't win when you're down a pawn. Of course, in tournament there's no taking back moves. Then there's time. You get sixty minutes to make forty moves. So you have to think reasonably fast."

Charlie looks to the street and rolls his sleeves up. He doesn't say anything for a minute then says, "There's better games."

"I'm going to go home."

"Fine. This is not enough fun for you. Sucking dick and making money is boring. I'll see you back there."

I walk away.

You push pawns. You measure time in squares across a board. You wait but the clock ticks so you force your move. Every Tuesday the chess team meets. Sometimes I go to a coffee shop by the lake and wash dishes for half an hour. In exchange they give me coffee and day old muffins and I sit and play with the Taxi Drivers when they get off of work. Secretaries half-dead with strung, beady eyes and strange wrinkled clothes read books and play games of chess and Go. The people are messy. They are messy people with wrinkled shirts and strung out eyes. But they know. You push pawns. You move the pieces. On Sundays at four a jazz band plays and then passes around a plate but nobody puts any money in the plate. We just push the pawns. The cafe has books lining the wall spelling out the history of jazz. On Wednesday there is open mic poetry. You push the pawns, you move the pieces. On Tuesday I am always better. Always one week better. I do homework, I study. I keep a notebook for my physics class. I read *Pride and Prejudice* in English. I go to the cafe when I'm not with Charlie and I push pawns. Sometimes I have too much homework. Other nights I go with Charlie, but less frequently. Charlie thinks chess is a game for people that can't play life. Charlie says he is absolutely sure of it.

The first time I beat Butterman he wipes the pieces to the floor and I tell him, "If you think I'm picking those up you are fucking crazy."

We visit other schools. Sullivan, Bauer, Senn. We win games. But I like best playing the Taxi Drivers at the No Exit Cafe where we measure time in square spaces and smoke until our lungs are sick. Where we drink coffee and eat crumbs off of tiny plates. I like playing chess until it is time to go home.

· · ·

The winter roils across Chicago like a cold broiler. It feels light coming in but the days are colder. Charlie and I feel it in the nights down on Addison. When I don't go with Charlie sometimes he comes home shivering.

Starla and I sit in the smoking room. Starla has a new ring on her finger. She got married two weeks ago.

Starla sits by the cold window and Ant has gone off somewhere.

Charlie is still in bed. This morning I sat with Phillip and tried to get him to talk to me but he would not. He is still sitting in his room. He has been there all day. Jonathan and Eric are off somewhere, probably building houses out of pebbles. I am sitting in the smoking room pouring my heart out to Starla. "I don't have any friends at Mather."

"You'll make friends," Starla tell me. That's Starla for you, a nice girl. A peach.

"So far I've been beaten up and nothing else. I don't fit in."

"No one fits in," Starla says. "That's what makes us individuals." She sure can be hokey sometimes but I don't say so. I just smoke my cigarette. I pick up Ant's guitar and strum a few sad chords. I only know a few chords.

"How's it being married?" I ask Starla.

"It's wonderful," she says. I strum the guitar and try to make up some lyrics.

She's in love
Like a pink dove
In the summertime
We had a blast
But that time is past
And now she is looking for a place to fly

Starla claps and I nod my head. "If it doesn't work out between you and your dumb new husband you just let me know," I tell Starla.

"It'll work out, Paul. Life is nice that way."

"Everybody's got their theories."

The chess team at Mather does well. We beat the other crap city schools and then we get invited to go downstate. One day while playing Jessica, her finger brushes my finger as she snaps up my king's side rook. I let her know I'm just a group home brat and put on my best victim face. She asks me to come to her house for Thanksgiving.

On the first snow of the year the air fills with cold white flakes. They lie on porches and lawns like soft sheets of paper. They fill the grooves in people's hats, the wrinkles on their cheeks. Dirty, angry cars push down the salt-lined streets, traffic slows. The blue sky is dull and half-spotted with the long gray clouds. I follow Pete to his home. He lives in a nice enough house. There are no mansions in this neighborhood, but for the neighborhood it is a nice house. It is a bungalow with a round roof and the bricks are all brown. It is the kind of house that could always be tuckpointed. I give him a holler and he turns around and at first he looks surprised then he balls up his hands into fists.

"You follow me?" he asks.

"Yeah. Why? You got something to hide?" I walk up close to him. He is like an exhibit in the zoo. The last of the twentieth century Neanderthals. He wears a baseball cap and a layer of snow sits neatly on the cap. Thanksgiving has not come yet but a few cheap Christmas lights decorate some of the windows. "I got to tell you something."

"You better talk fast." He breathes heavy on my face. Our breath makes clouds in the air. His lips are red and swollen with blood.

"Listen," I tell him, "Take me seriously. The next time there are going to be people with me here. We don't care how tough you are. We will wait for you with bats around corners. You will never be any kind of safe. You will have to travel in packs of six. If I bring the group home to you, you are going to regret it."

"I'm not afraid of you," he says. "What's a group home? What makes you think we won't do the same to you?"

"You got your group and I've got mine. But I'm used to it. You follow me to my house, there's people there. Where are your friends right now?" It is a really cold day but Pete's hands are out of his pockets anyway. He seems to think we are going to fight right now. "Anyway," I say, "You don't have to believe me or be scared. I'm giving you a perfectly reasonable warning, after that, you roll your own dice." We stand face to face for a bit in front of his house. What do I have? Maybe Breen and Larry if I can talk them into it. What does he have? The entire football team. But it's true what I said. I'll hit him dirty. Hell, I'll burn down his house if I have to. Then I turn on my heels and walk away. He probably thinks I am crazy. I feel a little crazy, but better.

Jessica's got a bedroom straight out of a fairytale. A big, sparkling, white down comforter covers her bed. Fluffy white curtains hide the windows. The bed is made of wood and there is a wooden dresser and a small wooden desk with two drawers. On top of the dresser in steel frames are pictures of Jessica with her brother who is away in graduate school. There are pictures of Jessica holding her father's large hands and pictures of her father and mother together smiling. One has Jessica sitting in a cheerleader's outfit, posing for the sun. I kiss her mouth and she wraps her long arms around my neck. I trace her curves with my hands, slide my hands up the back of her shirt. She pushes me away and locks the door and takes her shirt off. The rest of her family is still eating their thanksgiving dinner. It was nice of her to have me over. She turns the stereo on and I kick my shoes off and sit on the bed. She comes to me and I suck on her nipples and touch her stomach. She doesn't resist me. I unbutton her jeans. I reach down inside her pants and it is like magic, all warm and soft. We kiss deep and I lie her down with a hand behind her head. She pulls my shirt over my head and I feel embarrassed for a second but she kisses me anyway. Then I think about her parents clearing the plates from the table. Jessica coaxes me inside of her and I come immediately and fall back on the bed drenched in a puddle of sweat.

"That's not supposed to happen," she says.

"What's supposed to happen?"

"You're supposed to be in me for twenty minutes before you do that."

"Twenty minutes!? I'll never make it."

"You have to. That's what you're supposed to do."

"It's too much. I need training."

"I'm only going to give you one more chance. Twenty minutes."

"Right now? I think I'm ready."

"No. Next time. Put your clothes on."

I get off her bed and pull on my jeans and shirt. I feel completely drained. "Can we go to sleep?" I ask her.

"My parents would freak out. After college we can get an apartment together and lie in bed all day."

There is a knock on the door and Jessica's mother comes in. She is shorter than Jessica but has the same large cheeks and has done nothing but smile the whole evening. "How are you kids doing?"

"Good," Jessica answers.

"Did you enjoy your meal, Paul?"

"I did. It was really good. I think it was the best meal I ever had."

"That's nice. Come again anytime. It doesn't have to be a holiday."

"I will. I hope to."

Jessica smothers me, holds me tightly. She doesn't want or need anything. Jessica is the first girl I have ever had sex with. In school we walk the halls through the crowds holding hands. We move easily without being bumped by shoulders, elbows or backpacks. After school sometimes we sit on the ledge in front of the building and she wraps her legs around me or lays them across my lap. Money I make sitting watch for Charlie or Candy I spend on getting Jessica cards and flowers.

Jessica's skin is smooth. Jessica is thin with small breasts. I stay clean-shaven for her and her parents. Her father owns a bar downtown and says when I am older I can bartend for him. Then he laughs and his wife laughs. Jessica's parents always laugh together.

Jessica likes to laugh. I dance for her in convenience stores. I read her poetry. I go to football games to watch her jump around in little blue skirts. The team plays outside of the school in the park. I never stick around after the games. Jessica says her mother is finishing her Ph.D. Jessica says daddy's bar is doing well. When her parents are not home we study together and I try to have sex with her. "C'mon," I say. "I'm going to make it twenty minutes this time." Sometimes she will, sometimes she won't. It's like she holds back until I can't take it, until I am ready to sign away my soul just to be able to sniff her legs. And then, when I'm so horny that I can't think straight, just at that point when all I can do is stare at the pages of my book blankly, then she takes me into her room and gives me anything I want and I am OK again. She smells like flowers in the winter. She says she doesn't want our relationship to be just about sex. The last time we had sex it ended with me curled up in a ball and her arms around me telling me everything was going to be OK. She said, "Just lie there, everything will be OK."

The cars come and go on Addison. The wind is like ice off the lake. "I'm cold," Charlie tells me. "Fucking cold." He hunches deeply in his jacket. I wipe the snow from the top of the newspaper rack. "You can't come with me anymore. Not until spring."

"Don't say that."

"I mean it. I'm going away for a few months. Somewhere warm."

"Charlie…"

"Look. Where are the girls? It's too cold, that's where the girls are. I'll see you in the spring. The winter is not worth it."

I dig into a patch of ice with a nickel.

"Don't be sad. You need time to work on your chess game. You've got school. You've got a girl. Something's got to give, right?"

"Guess so."

"Look at me." Charlie spreads his arm out. A car passes. "I am the wind."

• • •

It has gotten late, late in the holiday season. Late and Charlie is off in Florida or something. He should be staffed out but I haven't heard anything about it.

Christmas morning I pull the old ironing board out of the closet, stretch the legs. Tracy comes walking out of her room, fat puffy faced. She wears an orange and white robe. I lay my jeans on the board and press into them hard with the hot iron. "We could get you a pair of nice pants." She says leaning over me. She smells like soap.

"It's Christmas. Everything's closed." The steam rises off the jeans. My fingers are cold. Next I lay a long button-up white shirt on the board. The shirt goes to my knees but I will tuck it in.

"We could get you a nice shirt."

"I have to dress nice today. I have to go to church today." If I was going to give Tracy a nickname it would be Hands On Her Hips, Hands On Her Hips Tracy. She watches me do my ironing and follows me to the closet. I stand the board and iron with the dusty old boxes. A wind comes across my neck and one of the boxes goes to fall, then another. I hold them up, shore them in, but every time another box wants to go. More wind comes across my neck. "What?" I ask her. I don't turn around. I face all the boxes and the ironing board waiting for the worst. The boxes tremble. Her feet pad across the carpet back to her bedroom.

Some of the lawns have decorations, deer and green lights. Little baby Jesus plastic dolls. A soft snow borders the thick, clean walkway. Thousands of bricks layered with mortar built this house. The closer I look the more grades and colors I see, but when I pull back the bricks are all the same dull brown. I made excuses not to go to church with Jessica and her parents today. Jessica did not buy it. It is early. I count the bricks. My jeans are stiff and shirt tucked in deep. I count the bricks, stare at the brown wooden door. When Jessica opens the door she smiles. Jessica smiles all of the time. I hand her the gift-wrapped box and she kisses me quickly on the cheek. "Well, don't you look nice."

"Don't patronize me." I come in with her. Her parents are around the couch and her grandmother is here as well. We shake hands.

"I've heard you're a nice boy," her grandmother tells me.

"It's true."

Grandma sits up front with Dad, Ma sits in the back with Jessica and me. I sit against the door and Jessica sits in the middle. Ma smiles a lot and Jessica smiles a lot. Everybody smiles all the way to church. The church parking lot is filled with cars, green Hondas, blue Fords. The streets are empty but the church is full. We pile out of the car and join the crowds entering the building through the large white pillars. Inside, wooden pews run the width of the church, long rows of wood and stained glass windows frame the building. "Isn't it pretty?" Jessica whispers in my ear. Her hand touches my belt.

"I haven't been in too many churches, to tell you the truth."

Jessica's parents shake hands and say hello. Everyone is wearing a suit. People get dressed up for church. Perhaps they are bucking for a promotion. Perhaps God is handing out raises. Or maybe God is Santa Claus, dropping presents to the best dressed boys and girls. But what do they ask for? What do they ask when God is Santa Claus? Maybe they ask for intelligence or maybe blissful ignorance, a long sleep until death and then some gnarled up old priest can toss a shovelful of dirt on the whole lot of them. We all get seated and the priest comes out and starts talking. I bite at my nails and Jessica pinches my leg. I do not like the priest. I do not like his stiff clothes and his dumb white collar. Jessica wears a suit with a skirt and I watch her legs cross high in black nylons. I would like to get her right now, in the bathroom or something, while the flock is listening to the preacher. I would like to get her on the bathroom floor. I bet the bathroom of this place is spotless. I could probably stick her right on the bathroom floor and not even mess up my shirt. Jessica smiles at me and I smile back. The preacher is getting louder. "Some people think the Lord is not watching," he bellows. "But the Lord is always watching. Some people love themselves more than God but we must love God more than ourselves, the way that He loves us. We must try to follow in His lead." He continues but loses me. I am stuck on Jessica's thighs covered in nylons and imagining what it is going to take to get between them. The whole day with her parents. It is too much to bear. We all stand and sing something I do not know the words to. "If there is a God," I think, "put the words in my head." But the words do not come to me. "There is no God," I whisper under my breath. I keep staring at Jessica's long, thin legs. When I turn back her grandmother scowls at me. I try to look ahead but I can't keep my concentration. When the singing stops we all sit down and people go to the front to give thanks publicly. One of them says, "While I was praying the Lord came to me and said there is a new member in this church and to thank him and to tell him that He loves you and is glad you are here." The guy has short black hair and a striped shirt.

Afterward people stand around and people talk. The guy in the striped shirt comes to welcome me. "I saw you, I saw you coming in. I saw your face," he says into my ear. "I could see you doubting." Jessica's grandmother looks over at us.

"Doubt? No, not me."

"It is wonderful that you are here," he says. "This is where you belong, with your friends."

"Glad to be here," I tell him. He smiles, I smile back at him and turn the other way. When I turn back he is still there and I find myself asking, "You need something?"

"I just wanted to welcome you."

"On behalf of God?"

He nods and smiles. "That's right." He pulls a card out of his shirt. "My name's Jacob." He turns the card over in his fingers. "You can call me anytime."

I tear his card in half. "You're a sick fuck," I whisper to Jacob.

Jessica saddles up next to me. I feel her fingers. The flock swells towards the center. The wooden pews empty and the spaces along the sides and the middle fill like water. A big smiling river of happy faces. I touch Jessica's leg, fingertips. While whispering in her ear I see her grandmother talking furiously to the man in the starched, striped shirt. People push politely past one another and then back again. The church breathes, people rise in tides and wash up on the shore. The hall fills with "hello" and "pleased to meet ya." I start to go black, cloudy, too many people. I try to squeeze out until I finally burst out of the doors of the church and throw up into the snow catching the pillar for support.

"What's wrong with you?" Jessica wipes my mouth with a napkin.

"I must have eaten something wrong."

We sit on a bench and the churchgoers come out and everyone waves goodbye. Jessica and I hold hands and her parents and grandmother come out. The cars leave one at a time and the parking lot thins. Jessica's dad runs his fingers through his hair. "You feel better?" he asks.

"I feel great."

At Jessica's home large plates of food are laid out on the table. Turkey, ham, deviled eggs, mashed potatoes, stuffing mixed with bits of apple and bacon, sweet potatoes covered in marshmallows and salad topped with pepper and oil. Jessica's father says grace and we eat. My stomach has settled and I eat as much food as I can.

We sit around a Christmas Tree opening presents. Jessica gives me a silver necklace, I give her a snowman in a glass bubble holding a sign that reads Winter 1989. We get presents from her parents. Jessica's parents give me a light-blue sweater from The Gap and I tell them it is the best present I have ever got and Jessica opens her presents from her parents, which include clothes and books and CDs and gift certificates. They open their present from her, which is a plaque that reads, 'Greatest Mom And Dad In The Whole World.' Hugs are given all around and we all have a glass of wine, even Jessica and I. When no one is looking I dip my hand into Jessica's father's jacket pocket and pinch a twenty-dollar bill. After all of that Jessica's parents leave to take Grandma home and have a brandy with some friends on the other side of town. Jessica has already changed into blue jeans and a T-shirt, my white shirt is out of my pants and looks like a dress.

We take our clothes off in her bedroom and kiss naked by the dresser. I knock over a picture and stop to pick it up. We kiss again and I feel between her legs. She is warm and her skin soft and smooth like a piece of fruit. She lays me down and ties me to her bed with pairs of tights. She sits on my stomach and touches my face lightly.

"Do you love only me?" she asks.

"I do."

She kisses me hard on the mouth then lifts herself up and lowers herself onto my face. It is only her I can touch, taste, and feel. Only her I smell and see. Jessica envelops me, surrounds me. I lose myself in her, in her sensations, motions. I drown in her. I don't hear myself crying, her moving. I lose breath. I feel the friction along my cheeks. Feel the tiny hairs with my tongue, taste her, I try to get out of me and into her as best as I can. I cannot hear her hum but I can feel her move. I cannot hear myself begging, "Don't stop." I feel the bed beneath me like a concert. I do not know how much time has passed or who I am. She unties me and I curl up like a bowl. She strokes my head with the tips of her fingers and tells me it's time to get up. She runs her fingers through my hair and I crawl, closer into her. There is no space outside this room, no world beyond these walls. I smell her skin, her arms. My head lies on her naked legs. No other place for me to go. I should always have been in this room.

"Get dressed," she says. I bury my face in her stomach, my legs over her legs. She holds me and I curl up tighter. I bury myself in the smell of her stomach. "Get up."

She kisses me lightly on the cheek and I uncurl, dress, pull my pants on, my legs shake. In Reed the walls were white. What must have been a century ago? What happened to Jay and French Fry and

Mike? I sit on the bed half-naked, half in half out. In Reed the psychiatrist asks me if I am taking any medication. Jessica kisses me again, lightly on the cheek, to bring me back.

When her parents arrive we are sitting on the couch watching television.

"Anything good on TV?" her mother asks. Her father places a paper bag full of something on the kitchen table.

"Nothing much," Jessica says.

"Nothing much," I echo.

Her father wobbles out of the kitchen slightly knocking the garbage can. I stand to leave and shake hands with everyone and apologize for throwing up on their church.

Across the soft cold night of the neighborhood to my home the Christmas windows all sleep. I light a cigarette. Some of the bars are still open on Devon and the men inside, sad and sullen, sit over their beers. I blow clouds of smoke.

I step in guided by the blue glow of a neon can of Old Style. The men, beaten by their lives, eye me for a moment and say nothing. I order a glass of beer and lay the twenty I stole from Jessica's father on the bar. A fat woman with straw dry hair laughs on the end by the jukebox.

The bartender places a glass of beer in front of me. "You got any I.D., kid?"

"No," I tell him and take a drink of the beer. It tastes good. I'm going to have to get some income. "Give me a packet of chips."

The bartender throws a bag of chips at me. The guy next to me must be forty years old with his hair slicked back like a greaser and a face you want to punch. I drink my beer quickly and another one comes. I feel empty. I left my soul at Jessica's house. "Jesus Christ," the old greaser says. "Jesus, kid. You know what I do? No fucking lie. Jesus, kid. I'm a fucking chauffeur."

"That right?" I pull on my beer. Some new pants, a new shirt, that's what I need.

"You wouldn't believe the size of the car I drive. Fit a whole Mexican family in the fucking thing. A whole fucking family, you hear me?"

Someone hits the jukebox and a tune starts up, echoing the smack of balls from the pool table and electric rings from the pinball machine. The bartender stands listless at the end of the bar wiping down glasses. The bartender pours himself a shot of whiskey and drops it in his mouth.

"I've been driving for twenty years. Shit, Jesus, I was probably younger than you when I started driving that thing." His voice sounds like a rock hitting a tin can. Someone strikes a match and the smell of sulfur mixes with the smell of cheap beer and wasted lives. "Twenty fucking years, you hear me kid?"

I take a good swallow. The bar clock reads one a.m. "So what are you gonna do?"

"I don't know, kid." He runs his hand over his scalp until the scalp becomes his crisp, greasy hair.

The bartender lays shots of bourbon on the bar for everyone. "Merry Christmas," he says and glasses clink and we all sniff down our shots.

"You know what I want, kiddo? Jesus. Merry fucking Christmas man and I love you and all that shit. What I fucking want is for some low budget asshole to chauffeur me around. I want somebody to open doors for me. That's why I fucking do it. I want someone to open doors for me, that's all."

We stare into our drinks. I feel pretty buzzed now and I hope I don't throw up again. First on a church and then in a bar. What a day that would be.

"Anyway kid, my name is Ed. That's all I'm trying to say. Jesus."

Someone slips some quarters into the pool table and the balls tumble down the rack cracking and knocking against one another. "No more fucking pool!" The bartender shouts. "We're closing this place in twenty minutes in case you don't know. It's the law!"

I drink down my beer and stumble off my stool. "Jesus, kid, you're fucking wrecked."

Ed drives me through the neighborhood in the biggest limo I have ever seen. At the house he opens the door and I fall out into the snow. Ed helps me up and to the door where Tracy lets me in. She trips me in the hallway and I fall on my face. "That's a nice car you're driving these days."

"Hell yeah," I tell her. "I'm fucking rich."

Phillip and I walk down Pratt Avenue to the Quick Stop. We pass houses and a grammar school and a frozen water fountain. Tracy told us to get cheese for dinner. She wants to make a lasagna. "I have this relationship," I tell Phillip. He doesn't say anything, he just holds the money in his fist. "C'mon Phil, why don't you say anything?" But he doesn't. "You haven't spoken in months. You keep it up and they're going to lock you up. It's not a good thing. Trust me." Phillip shrugs and even smiles a little. "Fine. Anyway, I have this relationship. You'll see, when you're older like me. I'm 17 years old. When you're my age you'll see what girls can do to you." Phillip is a good listener.

An old man in torn brown pants stands outside of the store. His face is rough and his nose red with cold and liquor. "Don't feed the fucking pigeons!" he says. "You feed the fucking pigeons I'll catch one, rip his wings off and throw him in your fucking face!"

We go in the store. Rows of cans line the walls and three video games stand by the newspaper rack. "You like Chef Boyardee?" I ask Phillip. "I love that stuff." We grab a packet of mozzarella cheese and a green can of Parmesan. I eye the video games beyond the magazine rack. The Indian guy behind the counter rings it up. He eyes us suspiciously so I smile for him and pat Phillip's head.

Outside the old man starts up again. "Go back where you're from!" he yells.

"Fuck you. Ain't you got a home?"

He huffs the snow from his bright red beard. "I'll tell you something kid. They'll get you again kid. They'll get both of you. You think they won't but they always do. They always get you. And next time you won't be so lucky! So don't feed the fucking pigeons!"

I ball up some snow and throw it at him and hit him in the head. He chases Phillip and me down the street screaming but we are faster and get away from him with no trouble at all. We bolt down the alley off of the playground. I knock over a garbage can and Phillip jumps up and down on the lid. We come to our steps and before going back in I say to Phillip, "Wasn't that fun? Every year better than the last." We walk inside.

Jonathan, Ant, Eric and I watch from the living room as they take Phillip away. "Why are they putting him in that car?" Jonathan asks.

"Because he's a pussy," Eric says. I backhand Eric and he glares at me.

"He should have said something," Ant says. Eric wipes blood from his lip and spits at me. I wipe the spit on the back of the couch. The car's red hood shines in the snowbanks. We all wait for Phillip to bang on the windows.

"Where are they taking him?" Jonathan asks. I shrug and look to Ant. Ant raises his hands. Starla comes in. "Where are they taking him?" Jonathan asks.

"Somewhere nice," Starla says.

"Bullshit alert," Eric says.

"Yeah, that's bullshit," I say. Starla smiles. The car drives away. Phillip is gone.

"What the fuck, Starla?"

"I'm sorry," she says. "We all liked Phillip."

"Not me," Eric says. "I never liked him."

"That's not the point," I say. "They just came and took Phillip away. Do you know how fucked up that is? That is totally fucked up. They shouldn't be able to just come and take people away. Where are his parents? Who's defending him." Nobody says anything. "Man. This place is wrong. They're going to take us away one at a time."

Starla looks like she's going to cry. "Well," I say. "What are you going to do when they come to take us away?" She covers her face and walks out of the room. "Don't tell anybody they took me somewhere nice," I say after her.

Ant and I split to the smoking room.

"I'm thinking a tattoo," Ant tells me.

"I can give you one. All we need is a pin and india ink. That how I got mine."

Ant lights two smokes and hands me one. Ant runs a finger down the middle of his face. "That's a bad idea," I tell him.

"I'm a freak," he tells me.

"You're not a freak. You have long hair and listen to heavy metal. You smoke pot and you don't like school. You have to be the most normal guy I know."

"Maybe you don't know me."

"Fuck you. I know you better than you know yourself."

He runs his finger down the middle of his face again. "Two sides to every coin," he tells me.

"You'll regret it. It's never too late to quit but it's always too late to start. You've only got another year here. All you have to do is make a couple of good decisions."

"All the good decisions have been taken." Ant blows a cloud of smoke. "All they left were the bad ones."

"Two Answers," I say to Jessica. The streets are thick with ice and snow. I nearly fall but grab her fingers and she keeps me up.

"Two Answers?"

"Yeah. You know. Just something bad that's happened to you."

She thinks for a bit and doesn't say anything at first. Then she says, "Nothing bad has ever happened to me."

We turn the corner. We've walked around the block three times. I don't have any money to do anything. She's got some money but she doesn't want to spend it on me. Her lips are bright red and her white skin highlighted by the cold. "What do you mean? Of course something bad has happened to you. Something bad has happened to everyone. Weren't you ever raped?"

"No."

"Beat up?"

"No."

"Abortion?"

"No."

"Death in the family?"

"No death in the family."

I feel silly. I've told her everything but this is the first time I have ever asked her any questions. I told her about my mother dying. I told her about my grandfather's throat rattling and I just happened to be the only one in the room and how I didn't tell anyone, I just let him die. I told her how I had a friend named Justin who I cared for deeply who got assfucked by a big black truck driver while I was sleeping in the cab in East Los Angeles. I told her about my nights on rooftops and hotel rooms filled with men and cocaine. I even told her about running away with Tanya and how we were caught sleeping in a tool-shed and they had come and taken Tanya away. She never commented on Tanya except to say that, "She sounds nice." I told her about being handcuffed to a pipe, about my father's obsession with shaving my head. Every time I told her something more she held me tighter, told me we would be OK. Only now do I see what a fool I am, what a selfish fool. Selfish fucking bastard.

Jessica grabs my hand. "I've got a lot of anger," I tell her.

"You have to let go of it. You have to get over stuff."

"Sometimes I'm not sure if I've ever gotten over anything." This time we cross the other way. Start circling the other block. "Nothing wrong, nothing bad happen, ever? Your parents ever fight?"

"Not really. If my mother wants anything bad enough she screams and my father always gives in. He's a big pussycat."

"So what the fuck is life to you? What do you think about? What do you struggle for? What do you do with your fucking time?"

"Don't be mean."

"It doesn't make any sense."

"I'll leave if you're mean."

"I'm sorry."

"You're not defined by your problems," she tells me. "You're defined by your solutions."

I think about it for a second. "That's the dumbest thing I've ever heard."

"Fine, I'm leaving." She turns and walks back along the white side-walk. I watch her go for a minute before chasing after her.

"Take me back," I say.

"Alright."

"You're awful good to me," I tell her.

"Why wouldn't I be?"

Tracy throws another manila envelope at me and walks away. "Something from the fat black guy?" Ant asks. I shrug my shoulders and open it up.

Paul,

I ask only one thing, that you love only me. I'm not allowed to talk too much about the policies but life here is not fun. I miss the time we had together. I remember sleeping in the toolshed and that night it was raining and you cried. I've always liked the rain. The clouds are like blankets and people can't see each other so well through the drops. I like the way the streets get all shiny afterward and how the air smells clean. When I hear the rain I think of you.

In here no one has a face. We are all black. We all wear the same clothes and use the same color toothbrush. The food is better than it was in the mental hospital and the smell is not as bad but everything else is worse. We don't really have social workers here, just guards.

I know I am being selfish when I think about you. I want you to love me more than I want you to be happy. I hope you understand. I know that I would rather be unhappy with you because I could never be happy without you. One day I am going to be sitting on your doorstep and we can be happy or unhappy again. Please think of me.

Love,

Tanya

"What's wrong?" Ant asks.

"What's wrong with you?" I reply.

• • •

The winter lays into Chicago like a bulldozer. Chicago is a flat, white wasteland. Chicago is full of snow and news shows reporting the dead in the nursing homes. They're calling it a repeat of The Blizzard of '79. The police round up the homeless on Lower Wacker Drive and stuff them into heated shacks where they sit bolt upright under blankets. It is all on the news. The mayor says he is taking care of the problems. Stretchers carry the stiffs into vans. People say it is the coldest winter on record, same as they do every year. A kid at Mather is arrested for driving down Lower Wacker Drive and shooting a bum with a crossbow. We watch the news on the couch. There is more room without Phillip and Charlie.

The first days of the new semester are canceled due to the cold. The flakes swirl outside of the windows. Snowdrifts line the curbs and men come with shovels to dig out their cars. The cold consumes Chicago for weeks, the city shuts down. We sit in the living room watching the news shows. The streets are frozen.

The curtain lifts. On January 23rd we go back to school. "Glad to be rid of you," Tracy says. We get tokens for the bus because of the cold. The four of us march down to the bus stop and get on the big green bus with the other kids. They recognize me, but they look at Jonathan and Ant and Eric hard. The other kids think they are new, think that someone must have just moved into the neighborhood. They are wrong. We get off the bus at Peterson and Ant and the others go to the right and I join the herd to the left, powering across the street and through the park.

Jessica grabs me in front of the school and kisses me on the mouth. She holds me but I cannot feel her skin through her big green jacket. "I need you," I tell her. "When can we be alone?"

"Hmm, let me think." She puts a finger to her lips. Someone bumps me, then someone else. We follow into the school. We get pulled along in our raft.

Pete saddles up. He gives me a smile. Jessica's face turns black for a second. "Hey Jessica, you coming to the party?"

"Yeah. Of course."

"How you feeling, Paul?" Pete says to me.

"Pretty good, Pete." Pete laughs and ambles off. "What party?"

"It's a cheerleader party."

"Where?"

Jessica doesn't say anything. I reach in the pockets of my jeans for something. "Isn't it strange how we let each other down?"

"Pete's house."

"That right." I pull my pocket inside out and Jessica hangs her jacket on the hook in her locker. She wears a tight sweater that accentuates how skinny she is. "Talk to him often?"

"We're friends."

"He ever stick it to you?"

Jessica's soft, happy features firm up. Her face tightens. Lockers closing rumble down the hall. "I didn't know we were married."

"What makes you think that? Is that the way your father talks to your mother that makes you think that? They talk about fucking a lot? Is that what married people do?"

"Why don't you just come to the party then if you're so jealous." The halls have emptied now. Classes have started.

"Look, Jessica." I motion to the insides of my pockets turned inside out hanging out of my jeans like white floppy ears. Jessica clicks her locker closed and walks away and I watch her walk away and I want to walk away with her but I can't. Instead I just lean against the locker and she walks, walks away until she is inside a classroom and I am alone, against a locker, in the hall.

In physics we are all welcomed back. We draw charts. We try to prove things. We draw in our science pads. After physics there is a fire in the auto shop and they evacuate the school. We stand outside hugging ourselves freezing, waiting to go back in. Inevitably we do.

"Why don't you get a job?" I'm sitting at the living room table reading *Jane Eyre*. I look up at Tracy.

"I'm not bothering you."

"You're bothering me just sitting there."

"I'm doing homework. It's what I'm supposed to be doing."

"Why don't you have any friends?"

"Why don't you stop bothering me?"

"It's because you're unsociable. You don't know how to communicate with people."

"You call yourself a person?" I try to read more and I take notes. It is a boring book, no sex, no violence.

"You make me sick."

I close the book. "OK, I'm leaving. I have a party to go to anyway."

"I bet you do."

Ant comes down the stairs. "You want to go to a party?"

We walk the city, the same route. On Bryn Mawr and Campbell the Royals hang out in front of the ice cream shop with paint on their faces like clowns. They laugh at us when we walk by. We are on our way to Spaulding House. "Where are you going?" one of them asks, six feet tall, a baseball bat in his hand.

"We're going to Spaulding House to pick up Breen and Larry," I say.

"Oh." They all just stand there. "That's cool. People or folks?" He flashes a sign and grins from ear to ear so people won't hate him when he dies.

"We're just going to pick up Breen and Larry."

"Well tell my boy Larry, Lil' Ogie says hi."

"I'll be sure and do that."

We turn left on Spaulding and Spaulding house sits in the middle of the dark block. The house is round with cracks layering the stairs. Breen and Larry come on out like superstars on parade. "Your boy Lil' Ogie says hi."

Larry smiles big, shows his big white teeth. "You're one scared-ass white boy to act so tough," he tells me. "You know that?"

"Don't make me break your leg again," I tell him.

"So whose party is this?" Breen asks.

"It's a cheerleader party."

"How the fuck you get invited to a cheerleader party?"

"I live a charmed life. Everything always works out in my favor. Think your boys want to go?"

"Of course. Those niggers ain't got nothin' to do."

Pete's house is lit up. A few football players sit on the front steps. Music floats out of the house. Someone pisses on a tree. I show up with Ant, Breen, Larry, and six ogres dressed in clown makeup carrying baseball bats. We walk through the front door. Jessica sits on the couch talking to a friend. The music skips a beat. My friends go off to find some beers and something to break.

"What are you doing?" Jessica asks me.

"You invited me."

"I didn't invite you to bring a bunch of goons."

"What do you care? It's not your house." Jessica scowls at me. "Are you protecting Pete? You want to keep his house pretty?"

"What's wrong with you?"

I stuff my hands in my pockets. Pete's house has brown carpet and paintings of fruit on the walls. I feel bad. "Don't you love me anymore?" I ask her.

"Of course I do." I look around. People are nervous. Things are quiet. When she says it she sounds like she means it but she doesn't reach out to touch me. Maybe she worries what people will think. She's keeping something from somebody. She wants me to think she loves me and she wants other people to think she doesn't.

I grab a beer from a tub in the kitchen. Pete is there with a couple of football players looking angry. "I'm going to kick your ass," he whispers in my ear.

"Relax," I tell him.

We stand on the white linoleum with yellow imprints. He reminds me of the fights I used to have with Mike in the mental hospital and for a minute I feel grown up and mature. Pete holds a beer in his hand. He stands four inches over me.

"You didn't have to tell me about this party."

"I wasn't telling you. I was telling Jessica."

"What? Do you think I don't exist? I was standing right there. She's my girlfriend."

"Maybe you're not her only boyfriend."

I consider hitting him or smacking the beer out of his hand. A couple of Royals walk through with cups full of beer. "How you feelin' Holmes?"

"I'm good," I tell them.

"Yo'. Where all those fly bitches at?" I shrug my shoulders.

I turn to Pete and jack my thumb towards the gang members. "I'd like to say they're no different than me and you but it's just not true. What we have most in common with them is animal, you know." Pete stares at me with red, angry eyes. "Look, I would say wait a bit and then call the police because at some point, if my judgments are correct, these goons are going to destroy your house unless you make nice with them. Still, they'll probably destroy your house anyway." Larry and Breen walk in the kitchen with Ant.

"Hey guys. This here's Pete. Pete says he's been sleeping with my girlfriend. It's his house."

"Nice house," Breen says.

"I'd kill a motherfucker I thought he was messing with my girl," Larry says.

"You got a girl?" Ant chimes in.

Jessica has left the living room and I find her downstairs at the pool table with a couple of other girls and two drunken football players leering over her.

"Have you been messing around with Pete?" I ask her.

"We kissed once over New Year's but we didn't have sex."

"Did he see your ass?"

She folds her arms over her chest and scowls.

There is a keg in the corner and I pour myself a beer. "But you said you loved me."

"I do love you." Her friends wait for her to take a shot. "Look. If you don't want me to mess around with anyone else I won't."

I drink my beer and leave.

• • •

The phone rings somewhere in the house. I sit up in bed. The sun plows through the window. A tap comes on the door and Starla steps in. "It's two p.m., Paul."

"It's Saturday."

"You have a phone call."

I pull my blanket off and walk downstairs. Ant has already gone off somewhere. "Hello."

"Hi." It's Jessica and the sound of her voice gets inside of me. The first thought that runs into my head is, "I love you." But I hold the words back. I can't believe how sunny it is outside. The sun reflects off the big sheets of snow. It looks like we've been invaded by aliens. "So you want to know what happened last night?"

"Sure."

"Your friends broke two of Pete's windows and beat up some kid and then the cops showed up. You left just in time."

"Seemed like a good time to leave."

"Do you miss me?"

"Already," I tell her. We hold for a moment. "I miss you like you've been gone for years. I miss you like something I've lost forever."

"Oh, Paul. I don't know why I test you. Let's never be bad to each other again."

"When you say 'let's' do you mean let us?"

In early February the chess team goes a hundred miles south to the state tournament in Peoria. We take a red van down on the 55 South. I sit next to Jessica the whole way.

We play suburban schools with more money and smarter kids but we hold our own. I try to reconcile with Jessica between games over crackers and cheese but our communication is stilted.

At night all of the boys sleep in one room, Mr. Dell in another, and Jessica gets her own room for being a girl. "Sneak over," she whispers to me, but I don't. We place sixth in the tournament and we get a little trophy and the principal makes an announcement over the speaker.

In late February Charlie comes home. He walks up the stairs thinner and less pretty and less innocent but still alive. He has been staffed out but Tracy takes him back and doesn't say anything. I go to see him in his room and he says, "Don't worry. We'll be back in business soon enough." Late at night I hear Tracy and Charlie talking in her room with the door closed tight to keep the air in.

• • •

As spring eats away the snow on Chicago's streets, licks the roofs of the houses, defrosts the glass on the car windows, I do well in school and the head of JCB invites me downtown and buys me lunch and tells me how proud they are of me. He takes me to a building downtown with a giant blue mural of a gateway with mermaids wrapped around the arches.

"Paul, we're very proud of you. You have really turned it around."

"Thanks."

"And you know we have a scholarship fund."

"That right?"

"Yes. Up to now it's been used primarily for the children of employees but it was set up for you. You get into college and we'll make sure you're able to go."

"Sounds like a pretty good deal."

He smiles large for me. "It's not every day that someone from the homes goes on to college."

"I haven't even applied yet."

"We'd like to make a video out of you. You are a success story."

"If that's what you want." I drink the Coke he bought me. He places his large hand on my shoulder.

"I want you to think of me as your father. You should call me if you need anything." He takes a card out of his wallet and writes down his home phone number and hands it to me.

As spring comes and the homeless return safely to blankets under Lower Wacker Drive and the emergency shelters empty their litter, the chess team stops meeting. Our small trophy sits in a glass case next to the principal's office. Ant tattoos a blue line running down the middle of his face. Charlie comes home less and less. As spring comes children once again make the big decision to run away, to roll the dice and take their chances. As spring comes and the boards come off the abandoned buildings and policemen stumble across the dead frozen bodies of last year's runaways locked in love's embrace against the elements, the policemen stumble across the bodies of last year's runaways, as spring comes, as spring comes…

I skip a rock across the canal and a rat darts beneath a broken stick along the edge. The trees shadow this spot down near the water, the empty beer cans, the dead lighters and gum wrappers. I set to cleaning for a minute, tossing the old cans in a dirt pit, piling up cardboard from beer cases, but I wear out quickly and just sit up in the branches waiting for a boat. And when the boat doesn't come I make my way home. Cars drive by on Kedzie Ave. just the other side of the trees making the sound that tires make on the street in the first days of spring.

I never expect these things. Life is stranger than any book I have ever read. The spring has started and nearly three years have past. Tanya sits on the porch of my home while the sun goes down behind the three flats, the grammar schools, the convenience store. Tanya sits on the porch, her legs slightly spread, her hands in her lap.

"Your skin is so dark." It's the first thing that comes to my mind. She peers at me. Three years is a long time.

"You sound so mature."

"Maybe I'm getting old."

"Maybe I'm getting blacker," she replies.

I sit with her. She sits on the ledge and I sit on the steps. The lights go on in the house next door and for a few moments we hear swearing and threats and a pot falls to a floor. Then the lights go off and it is quiet again.

"When'd you get out?" I ask her. It seems like a reasonable question but she makes a sad face when I ask. She looks the same; she looks older. She looks so much older. Same nose, same mouth, same pitch-black skin, same breasts, same ill-fitting clothes. Old old old.

"You said you would take care of me." Her hands rest on her knees. Charlie comes walking across the street, his eyes spinning circles, walking hard on full tilt. He passes between us, his thin blue jacket unzipped; he stumbles up the stairs.

"Hey Charlie, you got a smoke?" He tosses a pack at me and bangs through the front door. I move around. I can't get comfortable.

"I can't get comfortable," I tell her and she shrugs her shoulders and pouts a little

"I'm 18. They tried me as a child. So when I turned 18 they let me out with a lot of provisions. Counseling, check-ins." When she speaks now she lies. She doesn't lie about the details but she lies. How could they ever try her as a child? She's a million years old. Almost three years ago some cops dragged her screaming from our toolshed paradise. "You failed me completely," she tells me. "I was raped by prison guards. The other girls pulled my hair out."

I pat my jacket down for matches. "Maybe we weren't ready."

"I never lied to you. I never let you down."

I try to strike a match but it won't light until I finally force it into the concrete stair and scrape it violently across the concrete with my thumb. When it lights it burns my thumb but I get a cigarette lit and then I stick my thumb in my mouth to ease the pain.

"Don't suck your thumb," she tells me. "You're not a child."

"Let's walk."

We walk through the neighborhood without saying too much.

"Why didn't you write me more?"

Tanya stares at the ground. "I couldn't. They would only let me write to family so I had to include letters to you in letters I sent to my cousin and then I had to hope that he would bring them to you. I didn't think he would."

"That's a lie. You should have told me where you were so I could write you back."

"You know about lies," she says. "Anyway, I never believed I would get out, even when they said I would. And I was afraid if you knew where I was you wouldn't come. And if I told you where I was and you didn't come it would have killed me."

"I looked for you everywhere. I looked all of last winter. I went all over. I checked in Reed and in the Juvi Hall on Hamilton. I even went to the Robert Taylor Homes. Nobody knew where you were."

"They knew. They just weren't talking." She kicks a stick. "I dreamed you were looking for me. I was afraid you had fallen in love with someone else."

I don't say anything. My silence is like a confession and one tear drops from Tanya's eye and rolls over her nose. She was afraid I had fallen in love with someone else. The silence continues like an argument. The silence goes back and forth, neither side making sense, bickering and angry, hurt, hurting. Finally the silence wears itself out, tired of arguing, the silence reconciles, not quite forgiving but recognizing its own futility.

"I don't care if you loved someone else. I don't want to know."

"Where are you staying now?" I look away. I want to change the subject. I don't want to talk about faith and promises. I don't want to talk about love. Love is a moving target. I wait for her answer. She rubs the back of her hand along her cheek.

"I'm with my cousin on the West Side," she tells me.

"Got a phone?"

"No."

I nod. We pass through the park, through trees, past water fountains, and around a small hill. A couple of kids sit on a bench passing a joint back and forth.

"How can I get hold of you, then?"

"You'll just have to make plans and stick to them. Can you stick to some plans? Can you make a date and be sure to show up?" She holds and releases her sentences as if she was swearing at me.

"Yes."

"Well, that's how then."

I take her hand in mine. The sun is almost all gone and I walk her towards the train station.

"I'm glad you made it," I tell her. "I've never seen anyone make it before."

"Yeah. I made it. But you know, I'm tired now all of the time."

We continue down Lunt Street. The evening is dusty and the air is full of small, puffy clouds. "I've been good, you know. I've been going to school. I'm planning on going to a university. I was on the chess team and we came in sixth in the state this year." Tanya runs her hand through my hair.

"You were always good."

We decide to meet next Sunday. I will come to her, on the West Side. At the train station we kiss on the lips and she hands me a tape. I examine the back. There are songs by The Blue Notes, Curtis Mayfield, The Coasters, Ahmad Jamal, Etta James. "I've never heard any of these guys."

"I made it from my cousin's record collection. I wanted to give you a tape of songs that made me think of you."

"What about these songs makes you think of me?"

"Every song I hear makes me think of you."

Tanya spins through the turnstile, up the stairs to the waiting platform. The vendor slams the wooden slats down over the front of his store and jams the lock shut. I finger the cassette tape and step out to the wind and cover my chest with my arms and walk home with my head down letting the cracks in the sidewalk show me the way.

Jessica and I stay late at school working on our college applications. Our test results came back. She did better than me but I get to check the little box that says, "Ward Of The Court," so I look good on quota.

Jessica thinks we should apply to the same schools. We fill out applications for Northwestern, University of Illinois, and University of Chicago, as well as for schools on the East Coast that I have never heard of but that Jessica says are good schools. Jessica says she likes New York. Jessica says she likes Washington, D.C. At eight o'clock they kick us out of the school and we pack up our papers and grab our bags.

"You're not the same with me." She grabs my hand. The grass is wet and gets inside my shoes. "It's because of Pete."

"I guess so."

Jessica squeezes my hand. "I'll never be with someone else ever again. Ever. Only you." They're beautiful words and I swallow them. I feel her soft hand, long fingers, look into her face. Her face is clean, unmarked.

I meet Tanya at Western on the Lake Street line. My fingers bleed from biting. It's a brutally ugly train station. All of the lights are broken. Junkies lie against the wood and try to grab my pant leg when I walk by. A large man stands next to the big red alarm button like he's daring me to push it.

"Look how pretty you've become," Tanya says touching my face. "What happened to all of that acne? You're pretty and you're thin."

"I didn't realize I've gotten thin."

"You have. You look like a movie star. You just need a haircut and you could be a model or something."

"I have issues with haircuts. My father used to shave my head."

"I know. But you can't let the past rule your future." We kiss on the lips. "I've been answering phones," she tells me. We walk up the back of her building. She lives in the deep West Side, the Wasteland. They call it the Wasteland because when Martin Luther King was killed this is where they had the riots. They burned all the buildings down. Every other building is a vacant lot. Pushing on the banister a large chunk breaks off and falls two stories. "Don't fall and hurt yourself," she tells me.

Tanya pushes the back door and we walk into a kitchen. The kitchen is clean. Tupperware lines the counter. The fridge is an off-yellow. "Beer?"

"Sure."

She hands me a Miller. In the living room an enormous man sits on a deep brown sofa watching a TV set. The TV is large and modern looking, heavily contrasting with the rest of the surroundings, which are clean but very poor. An old stereo stands four feet tall next to the entrance. "This is my cousin Ed."

"Hello, Ed."

Ed grunts at me and I follow Tanya into a bedroom. "So what do you mean you've been answering phones? I thought you didn't have a phone."

"We don't. My counselor got me a job. I answer phones in a warehouse. I'm a receptionist."

"You gonna work out of this?"

"Sit on the bed, get comfortable."

"OK." The bed squeaks. Out her window I can see the alley, and two men speaking casually, leaning over an old white car. I put my palms to the mattress.

"I'm going to get out. I don't know. I don't have a record." She sits down next to me and leans her head on my shoulder. She feels heavy. She needs me. "They have to erase your record. They say nobody is allowed to see it. I could finish school, get a better job. They say nobody could ever see. But if they did see they wouldn't believe it." She buries into me and I stroke her hair. Her hair is braided tight and it's dry. I can't help but compare it with Jessica's thick hair. I stroke her hair and her face, grab a drink off my beer and then stroke her some more. I want to stroke her to sleep, to stroke the years off her soul. I haven't been in The Wasteland in so long. I have forgotten how far gone this place is. Chances that Tanya would survive to this point, one percent. Chances that she would get out of here, less than zero. Her head goes down into my lap. Her thick legs curl up into the bed. She said I'm pretty. I've only ever wanted to be pretty. If someone would tell me I am pretty once a week for the rest of my life I could be happy.

I drink some beer. Tanya, I think, is napping. I try not to move too much. Out her window it's desolation for miles. A hotel with a pink light called "The San Remo" advertises rooms for rent by the hour.

Tanya uncurls still in my lap. She looks straight up at me. "I liked it better when you were ugly," she says. "Then I knew you wouldn't leave me because no one else would ever want you."

"That's selfish."

"I don't care."

"Go to sleep," I tell her and I rub her forehead. "Sleep away a bit."

I pull the blanket up around her, the blanket under her head. I grab my beer and head for the living room and Fat Ed. I sit on his couch on the other end of him. He wheezes loudly and eyes me and flips the channel with his remote. "Anything good on TV?"

"Never is." We sit for a bit. "There's never been a white boy in this house before."

"Would it help if I said I grew up a poor black child?" I ask him.

"That's a line of shit." More wheezing comes out of the fat bastard. "Tanya thinks you're some train full of gold passing through her station. To me you're just another white boy looking for some black cooze like the rest of 'em."

"Listen, you fat bastard. You don't know anything about me and Tanya." I grip the couch cushions and kill my beer. Fat Ed looks away from me towards his towering television set. I get up and grab another beer from the fridge.

"Don't drink all my beer, whitey."

"You want one?"

"Alright."

I bring him a beer. We sit for an hour and watch the television set. I go to the window and dig the action down on the street. There isn't much. A couple of guys working on an old car up on cinderblocks, a drained out crackhead walking in a hurry. A bull with horns passes and no one pays much attention. The cops are white, they don't want to get out of their car. The streets cannot accommodate them. And then I see it. It is sudden and awesome. I see that the city stretches forever. I see Charlie below the tracks on North hooking for tips and time and Ant in his room playing guitar far north by Pratt with a thin blue line tattooed down the middle of his face. I see south to the tip of the Taylor Homes where fires are burning and Willie has been killed. At Halsted and Maxwell, the near west, more junkies have moved in to take the place of Maria and Justin. The supply is endless. I see children's shelters funded by queers up on Belmont. Far West and

North hidden by trees and residential houses Reed Public Mental Health Facility takes up two square miles of city land. The city is immense. I see it in landmarks: The University of Chicago, The Sears Tower piercing the sky, Lake Michigan cleaning the city in the humid summers only so that they can freeze by winter's end. I see borders, I see Lake Shore Drive carving up the grass, the Dan Ryan Freeway carving up the South Side, keeping the blacks in the Taylors from killing the whites in Bridgeport. The whole thing makes sense for a moment. The whole city is planned, immense, and endless. The streets are a perfect grid. Millions and millions of people hide just how well constructed the whole thing is. There's a reason the ten-dollar hookers walk under the Lake Street El lines late at night. They are cheerleaders for the trains. Ten dollars is the perfect price. And it just goes on, measures out to the suburbs, busing the leaders into the Loop, busing the workers into a city they gave up on, they left to burn. The suburbs stretch for a hundred miles in any direction.

Tanya puts a finger on my back. The sun is going down and a man shuts the hood on an old Chevrolet. How long have I been here? The man looks up at me leaning out the window and winks. Tanya asks, "What's on your mind? You've been staring out that window for hours."

"I'm leaving."

"You're going home? It's not that late. You don't have to go."

"I'm leaving Chicago."

"When?"

"Soon as I can."

I turn and grab her and kiss her deeply. Fat Ed shouts something at the TV set, throws his remote at the wall. I hold her as hard as I can. It's all perfectly clear. I decide that the worst decisions are the ones you never make and I feel Tanya's arms holding me, holding me.

Ant, Starla, Charlie and I play cards in the smoking room. Charlie is my partner. I bid four books and Ant with his blue-lined face bids nil. Charlie calls it yard and Starla smiles and says, "Well, I guess we'll just go four."

"Board."

"What?"

"You'll go board, minimum, four."

"Yes, we'll go four."

After school I work on the forms using the library's typewriter. I write essays and reread and polish them. I secure recommendations from the principal and the head of JCB. I tell them I am just a normal kid trying to make good. I fill out forms; I send away for the necessary information. I work on it during my breaks, my lunch period. When I'm done I go home and do my homework while Tracy stares at me from the living room.

"You know what Jonathon is doing?" she says to me. "He's outside playing basketball. That's what normal kids do."

"I don't know if you noticed, but Jonathon is retarded."

Around eleven o'clock every night, about an hour before I gather up my papers Charlie comes through the front door. His eyes always spin. But Tracy never says anything to him. Tracy takes from him whatever it is she needs and lets Charlie go, eyes spinning, into the bedroom.

Charlie says, "Come with me tonight. I need you to watch for me."

"I don't know."

"I need you to watch. Just this one night."

"OK."

A breeze blows against the stop signs and neon lights. I sit perched atop my newspaper box biting my fingers while Charlie wavers near the corner. It's early. We are out early tonight. We don't have the protection of darkness. Candy walks by. "Where you been, baby?" Her skin is covered in a rash and the marks are poorly covered by cheap makeup. She is decomposing. She leans slightly to one side like she is about to fall over. Charlie won't even look at her. Candy walks away still saying, "Where you been, baby? Where you been?"

Charlie is wild-eyed tonight. He struts back and forth like a strange bird. He puts his hands on his hips and stares at me with one foot just in front of the other stretching out his skinny belly as far as it will go, puckering his lips. The sun has not fallen yet; an even, golden light illuminates all the wrinkles and worries on Charlie's landscape.

"You don't watch me like you used to," he tells me.

"Sure I do."

"No. With you now anything can happen. You have other things on your mind. Other loves, other plans."

A car horn sounds followed by the loud crash of a broken window. A man lies in a pile of glass across the street.

"It's not far away," he says like he reads my mind. "The other side of the street. Look at it. It's just a few feet away. Always is, you know." He touches my knee and I lean down towards him. "I don't believe in ugly people, Paul. For me they don't exist." He kisses me hard and I feel my mouth open and I feel his hand in my hair. I taste his mouth, it tastes like broken glass. His hand feels like the other side of the street.

When the car pulls up Charlie steps in easily even though it seems a long way off the curb. The shadows of evening come down like a slow curtain but they are too late. I see Charlie's cold blue eyes.

"Don't worry, Paul. Just follow things to their logical conclusion." And then the car is gone and Charlie with it. I will never hear from him again.

On Friday I am done. I pack my papers in my bag, books in my locker. Jessica waits outside the doors of the school. The spring blows her hair. She wears tight-fitting light blue jeans over her long legs. She's so damn pretty. "Hi stranger."

"Hi, Jessica."

"Join me for a cup of coffee?"

"Sure."

We walk over to the IHOP. Other kids are there from school. It's Friday night. We sit in a booth and Jessica orders two coffees. "Do you want some pancakes or something? Don't worry about money. I've got money."

"No. I'm OK."

"You don't eat enough." The coffee is hot and nice and wakes me up a little bit from my long week. "What have you been doing in the library everyday?"

"Nothing much. A couple more applications." Jessica stirs in some cream. She likes her coffee brown.

"I thought we were applying to the same schools."

"I just thought I would put some more out there. Just to be sure."

The waitress comes back around. "Do you want anything else?"

Jessica orders an omelet with bacon and cheese. To take up space on the table.

"You know," I tell Jessica. "The first time I ever was waited on I was twelve years old."

"Really?"

"Yeah. We never went out to eat in my family. If we did it was a burger and fries at McDonald's. It wasn't that the old man was cheap or anything, he just couldn't stand to wait."

"Are you impatient like him?"

"Not like him. If he had to wait in line he started talking to himself. He was crazy. He'd go off for any reason, or no reason at all. You wouldn't believe it. It was like living with a hurricane. That's why we couldn't go to a normal restaurant. We weren't poor. In fact, we had more money than any of my friends. So the first time I was in this restaurant with table service I just thought it was the coolest thing in the world."

"What was the occasion?"

"I was in a play and it was the cast party."

"You were in a play?"

"Yeah. I was in a play. I think my character was confused." I smile for her.

"I can see you as an actor."

"Thanks. I think."

Jessica's omelet comes and some toast and jam. "Have some," she says to me.

"That's alright." The omelet sits between us.

"What's happened?" Jessica asks.

"How's your family?"

"They're fine. They're in love."

"Still?"

"Isn't it great."

I drink my coffee and lean back in the chair. The orange plastic is blinding. Jessica continues, "Football season is over so I won't be cheerleading. I'll have a lot more time. I only ever see you in English class and you don't say anything, just run off down the hall."

"I don't know what's wrong, Jessica."

"I said I was sorry about Pete. You know, I put up with your flaws. If we're going to be together we have to make a commitment to work things out when they go wrong."

"What do you know about commitment?"

She goes dark again, takes a sip of her coffee, puts the cup down, picks up a napkin then throws it on the table with two fingers. "That's a cop out. You told me you wanted to be normal and have a normal life."

"I said that?"

"You did."

I rack my brain and remember. We were sitting at the kitchen table at her house. We were drinking orange juice and studying and I blurted it out. Her foot touches my leg.

I want to go home with her. I take a stab at the omelet and chew the eggs for a while. I want to go home with her because she holds me and tells me everything is OK, but I know it's a lie. I know everything is not OK. I want to go home with her because she represents everything I have ever wanted to be. She is smart, well adjusted, pretty. She loves her family. She is happy. I look at her and I see that her life will be a series of full steps forward. That even when she is old she will be beautiful and happy. I look at her and see that nothing could ever go wrong for her. Her family could be my family. She could protect me. I could hide under her shield. We could be happy happy happy. I want to go home with her and lose myself in her, to smell her. I love her smell, the feel of her skin. I feel like I will never stop thinking about her.

"I can't go home with you."

"Why not."

"Because if you lose me it won't kill you. You'll just get with someone else. You'll get over it easily. You don't need me, you're already complete. I need someone who is not complete because I am not complete. I don't know why, I just do. You could never be that person. You're too strong."

Jessica takes a drink of coffee. "You know," she says to me. "I hope you look back on your life and say to yourself, 'That was a really good decision.' Because you know what we could have? We could have a nice life. So I hope that whatever you end up with is better than that."

"Jessica, some decisions work out and some don't. It's a crapshoot."

She tosses her fork onto the plate and it makes a certain unforgiving, high-pitched sound.

This is not a big funeral. This is nothing special. There are no large black cars, women crying in big straw hats filled with flowers. There are no preachers, there are no friends. This is a small funeral, in a brick building on the northern end of a graveyard. My brother picks his nose and my sister sits in a white print dress with her hands neatly tucked into her lap. Her hair is combed and she looks like a picture hanging over a fireplace. Who knows what is on her mind? Her face doesn't move, her hands do not twitch. My stepmother wears a long, navy blue skirt, caramel-colored nylons, a firm grip on her face, claws wrapping her chin. She stands by a long thin window and the sky is a blanket of pale gray clouds.

This is not a big funeral. My father lies in some half-price casket in the center of the room. I am sitting on the end of a row of brown steel foldout chairs scuffing the tops of my shoes. I guess they expected a big procession. My brother's feet do not quite touch the floor. My sister's feet just touch the floor in black patent leather shoes. She is so polite. She could probably sit that way forever.

My brother squirms in his chair, moves around. He wants to go out and play, go run around, shoot some toy guns or something. I don't know him very well but I can tell that he doesn't like sitting still. He is like his father. My father could never sit still. He was always up and walking around, throwing things and moving from room to room, like he was running from the living room to the dining room but then he got scared of the dining room and ran back to the living room. When the storm ended he always came to me for forgiveness in the wreckage. When my mother died he blamed it on me, he handcuffed me to a pipe, he smacked me around, so I left. The police told me I had to go home, I told them to forget it. I slept on a rooftop for a year, warmed up at six in the morning in a yellow laundromat. I broke into basements and boiler rooms. I got drunk with other alley trash and laughed and talked about masturbation and smoking. I got caught sleeping naked next to a giant water heater. At some point I gave up. I crawled into an entranceway at a large apartment complex drunk and ready to die.

This is not a big funeral. My father lies in a box at the center of the room. He was not a good man but who is? When things hit him he took it hard. When my mother got sick he took it personally. He thought that he was the victim. He was less than a hero. When my mother was dying on the couch and pissing in a bucket on the living room floor he cried for himself. He screamed at me for not taking care of her. He screamed at her for not taking care of the children. He ran around with whores like my stepmother, and when my mother died he married my stepmother six months later.

He was not a bad man. He had a good sense of humor. He made money. He filled the freezer with steaks and the cupboards with cans of Chef Boyardee. He left me alone to do what I wanted as long as I did not get in his way. He left behind two beautiful blond-haired children. My brother has turned all the way around in his chair. My sister has a platinum streak in her hair. My stepmother stands by the window quietly eating her face. What now? She is a banker. She has loads of money. I was not poor growing up. We had a magnolia tree in the backyard. It was one hell of a magnolia tree. Paradise on earth. We had a stucco garage with a green roof. My father managed buildings. They have a giant house in the suburbs I have never seen. My father told me once it is four stories when you include the basement. He did not want to tell me where it was. That was his game. He said I could come and see it when I told DCFS that I was lying about being handcuffed to a pipe. He said I could come out and live in a big beautiful house in the suburbs. That I would have to tell them he did not shave my head or smack me around or yell at me and drag me out of bed at four o'clock in the morning. As soon as I would do that he would take me to his new palace in the suburbs and I could live with him and my stepmother and my little brother and sister. He should have told me the address instead of making me feel unwanted by not telling me where he lived. But I figure I was never cut out for the suburbs. I have always been a city kid, an alley rat. I like the streets in the city because they are busy. My father was not a bad man. He did not molest me. He did not beat me that badly.

My stepmother stands by a tall, thin window, arms crossed over her stomach. I admire her breasts. They poke through her starched white shirt. I would like to lay her here on the cold parlor floor, with the dust. Her hair is short and businesslike. Is this a business deal to her? She sent me a card letting me know about the funeral. She wears black shoes with tiny heels. My father lies in a box. His cheeks are sliding off of his face. His cheeks are freshly shaven. He wears a black suit but he is dead. He would never wear a suit when he was alive. I am not wearing a suit. I wear a cheap pair of blue jeans and a sweatshirt. My father was never one for dressing well. He bought his suits at the thrift stores, his socks at the Goodwill. I only have two pairs of pants and three shirts. My rich father has not funded my clothing. My clothing has been funded by the state, on a state-mandated clothing allowance. I do not have much in the way of clothes. I do not wear my rich father.

I admire my stepmother's breasts. I would give her everything I have to touch them, to suck on them. I swear, anything she wanted. I would promise her everything I ever make, everything I ever do. I suppose it would be impossible to seduce her. We do not know each other well and like each other less. Perhaps she would do it because I look so goddamn much like my dead father. I have the beginning of his wrinkles. We have the same large nose, the same forehead. She crosses and uncrosses her ankles. My sister sits perfectly quiet and it is becoming disturbing. She needs to move. It is not normal for a child to sit in the same position this long. But she just sits there. My brother gets up and tells my stepmother he is going to get some water. My stepmother says that will be fine.

We follow the casket out into the park. The cemetery is filled with small stones. It is a small funeral. There are no friends, no mourners. My grandparents are dead. The trees are all short. We follow the casket to a hole in the park and the box is lowered into the ground. I remember my father telling me emphatically that God doesn't exist. I do not believe he wanted to be buried with the dirt and the worms. He was not a bad man. We did not believe in Santa Claus. We were realists.

A priest reads something from a Bible, a long blue strap hangs from the end of it. My father was not Catholic. I think he was Jewish. My mother was British and belonged to some Protestant church. She was cremated. The group home I live in is run by a Jewish services foundation. My stepmother is Catholic. The wind blows her long dark blue skirt tight against her legs. I guess she is in charge now. She can raise the kids to be Catholic, send them to funny schools with nuns, dress them in polo shirts and pleated skirts. They will be fine. I hope they never have to know any better. The cemetery smells like any other park in the fall.

My brother looks bored, scared, restless. The priest mutters some words, "God's will. A good man dedicated to his family. Took care of his sick wife. Did not leave her." My sister stands close to the edge with her hands folded. My stepmother holds firmly to my brother. He looks like he is going to panic. He is getting ready to run. The priest continues but I shut him out and listen to the wind. In the wind I wish I had not been so hard on my father. I wish I did not drive him insane by hating him. I wish I said to him it was OK. I wish I said that I forgive him for being a lousy dad and I am sorry for being a lousy son. I would tell him that. They lower the box and the priest closes the book.

My stepmother drives a dark purple Lincoln Town Car with a velvet interior. My brother crawls in the back and my sister in the front. The door closes with the sound of the leaves falling from the trees. My stepmother starts the engine and the engine smoothes to life. She doesn't ask me if I would like a ride. She doesn't ask me if I would like to see their fancy house out in the suburbs. I guess it is too late for that. I missed my chance. There is no salvation in the suburbs. Pink clouds full of fire rain on the suburbs. My father wanted to show me his fancy house out in the suburbs. I watch them drive away, my sister looking straight ahead, my brother pounding at the back window. I stand on the corner next to an old wooden bench with a blue advertisement for Joey's Movers in front of an old corner store.

I push the door to the store open. An old man with white knuckles leans over the counter. I count the change in my pocket, forty cents and a bus token. I grab a pack of red gum.

"Thirty-five cents," he says.

I lay my change on the counter, grab my bus token, and walk out the door.

I see Tanya on Sunday. Her fingers are white and chalky with dead skin. "My father died," I tell her. Fat Ed looks up from his couch and snorts.

"I'm sorry," she says. She runs a dead finger over my cheek.

"Why are you sorry? He wasn't a good man. There's nothing to be sorry for." Tanya puts her hand around my shoulder, pulls me to her. I feel her breasts against me. "Why are you sorry?" Tanya holds me tighter. I keep asking, "Why, why are you sorry. People leave. I left him first. He called me terrible things." I stand still and Tanya holds me as much as she can. I stare past her, through tears. Outside the window I can make out kids walking through the lot, stepping on the weeds.

Tanya holds me. My arms rest at my sides. "I'm sorry," she says again, running her beautiful fingers through my hair, rubbing her face against my cheek like a sponge, trying to clean up the mess.

"My poor father," I say. "My poor father."

In English class Jessica and Pete hold hands. Pete smiles when he passes me in the halls, and I tell him that if he keeps it up I will bring more clowns over to his house and we will break all of his windows. I do my homework in the smoking room while Ant plays songs about losing people and I wonder how he fell so far. I guess some people who aren't supposed to make it do, and some people who are don't. The rest is just inevitable. I stare at the line tattooed down Ant's face, move to touch it, and listen to the sad, sad songs he plays.

As the school year comes to a close, the winds of summer roll across the parks and houses of the neighborhoods. On a Thursday I pick up Tanya. She steps out of the dusty warehouse, the men behind us staring at us, sitting on their forklifts with their sleeves rolled up, smoking cigarettes.

"C'mon, I have money," I tell her. "Let's get some ice cream."

She links her arm through my arm. "What's the special occasion?"

"I'll show you."

We grab a table at the ice cream parlor on 110th and Halsted and sit at the table in front eating sundaes with small spoons. I have chocolate and she has vanilla. Across the street is a fenced-in shopping mall, beyond that the Dan Ryan freeway roars.

"Up the street from here is Crossroads, a drug rehab. I had a friend in there once. A guy named Justin. I lost him in a truckstop in East Los Angeles." She places the spoon inside her mouth. "Like the way that ice cream dissolves in your mouth. That's how I lost him." The colors pop off the shopping mall; stern-faced security guards stand around in dull blue jackets. Tanya looks hard, like she has had a hard day, a hard life. "How's work?"

"I answer the phones but I don't have to lift any boxes." A gray Oldsmobile parks near the curb. We watch a silver-haired woman get out of the passenger side, carefully place her cane on the sidewalk. "What happens to all the people we pass in life?"

"I don't know. They come in. They make their mark, or not." She makes me think of French Fry, and now Charlie, who won't be home when I get back tonight. I put an envelope on the table. Tanya raises her eyebrows. "It's our ticket."

"Ticket to where?"

"I got into a school out West. We're going to California." Tanya pushes her spoon into her ice cream and lets it stick there. I move to touch her fingers and she pulls them away.

"What's that got to do with me?"

"You're going with me. We're going to get married and live in the married dorms with all the other nice married couples." She looks at the envelope and bites a spoonful of ice cream. "We're going to have a perfectly normal, happy life. I insist." She laughs and spits the ice cream onto the table. I laugh with her and knock my little cardboard cup full of ice cream to the ground. I choke on some ice cream and spit it to the sidewalk. We double with laughter, holding our legs. People walking by stare and one guy says, "That must be some good ice cream." When we are done we laugh some more until my stomach hurts and tears are in my eyes.

The last of the ice cream has melted to a sweet creamy soup. Tanya lives far away to the west and I have to go all the way north. We hold hands to the train station.

"It's a year away," Tanya says. "You still have a year of school." We purchase our transfers. We get some looks. People do not always approve of mixed couples. The train station smells of donuts from the small vendor to the left of the turnstiles. "You still have to finish. It may not work, you know." We stop where the stairs lead to the different tracks and I hold both of her hands and people walk around us. Her hands are cold with age and hard wrinkles. "It may not work."

"It may not," I agree. There is always that chance. The last three years have been long. I look into her face. "I don't ever want to spend three years without you again." The station is built of dark wood that separates into square views of a patched lot and some banged-up trashcans. I want to step back and see through the wood and get a clear picture of the world. I kiss Tanya to help me see it better.

• • •

Mother died hard. Some people die easy. They just die. My mother died for five years. She did not die well. She died on the couch paralyzed with Multiple Sclerosis, crying all of the time. She was not a liar. She did not say things were going to be OK. Once, I pushed her in her wheelchair to the movie theater. She cried the whole way home and swore she would never go outside again. My mother did not die well. Her skin melted into the couch cushions. She always lay back to prevent her head from falling forward. She was not courageous. Instead she would cry out loud how she could not wait for it to be over with. Her last years were filled with a simple misery and I'm as much to blame as anybody. I've heard it said that if you ignore a crime then you are the cause of the crime. I let my mother die, stayed away from her and her couch and the bucket full of piss that sat next to it. I let her die, only seeing her to bother her for money, yelled at her and even when she cried because she was dying and my father had told her she wasn't living up to her end of the bargain. I didn't feel her crying, even when she tried to grab me and cried into my shoulder as I thought of other things. I don't know why I didn't care more, I just didn't. I didn't really care. So of course she died. After her death the streets claimed me, the group homes, the institutions. And I became part of a lost group.

I try to crawl back inside and I struggle against the streets and the night, fight the weather, the alleys and the subway trains. All I've ever done is try to replace her. I didn't even know her but I have a hole inside of me and I can't imagine how it got there. Maybe it would have been there anyway, maybe I was born broken or maybe I was broken in transit. But there is no way to know now. I look across the lawn, smell the air for her ashes. I don't blame her. I can't blame someone for dying. I don't blame Dad either, or the state. I've just felt so alone these last couple of years and even when someone held me, I still felt alone. In fact, the more they held me the more I felt that way. I try to inhale any sign of affection. It keeps me weak.

I still smell the bucket that sat next to her bed. She was left without a headstone or a funeral. Her monument is just a shattered family of which I am the last remaining stone.

Gray clouds pull over the sky like a curtain. My mother's ashes were scattered in Udon Valley, England, so speaking out loud in a park in Chicago is not likely to do much good. A long jam of cars crowd down Peterson and I keep my head low and tune out the wailing horns. I walk past the record store and a closed-down niteclub that used to be called Moscow at Night. School is out; Tanya is getting off of work. She'll be waiting for me. The buildings are silent. They hide their secrets. Chicago is full of secret homes and treasures. Chicago is an army of six million boxes, bungalows, skyscrapers and two flats. Summer is rolling in but there is no heat, just a strong wind.

"I just want you to know," I say to my mother, I say to Chicago. "I just want you to know that I feel better now and I think things are going to be OK."

THE END

Acknowledgments

Thanks to Dave, Pat, Dorothy and Avril at MacAdam/Cage for the kind of basic humanity that is rare in life, to Annalise who proofread the book early when it was most needed, and especially to Molly and Susan Chehak without whom I would still be living in my car trying to figure things out.